ONE NIGHT
WITH MORELLI

ONE NIGHT WITH MORELLI

BY

KIM LAWRENCE

First published in Great Britain 2014
by Mills & Boon, an imprint of Harlequin (UK) Limited,
Large Print edition 2015
Eton House, 18-24 Paradise Road,
Richmond, Surrey, TW9 1SR

© 2014 Kim Lawrence

ISBN: 978-0-263-25607-9

Harlequin (UK) Limited's policy is to use papers that are natural, renewable and recyclable products and made from wood grown in sustainable forests. The logging and manufacturing processes conform to the legal environmental regulations of the country of origin.

Printed and bound in Great Britain
by CPI Antony Rowe, Chippenham, Wiltshire

Massive thanks to my editor Kathryn for
being so elastic with the deadline on this one!

CHAPTER ONE

SHE HATED BEING late and she was—very.

Her jaw ached with tension. Obviously it served no purpose to get stressed about stuff you couldn't control, like fog at airports, traffic jams or—no, dropping in at the office had been completely avoidable and a major mistake, but it was human nature and she couldn't help it.

Weaving her way neatly in and out of the crowds still wearing her sensible long-haul-flight shoes, Eve flicked open her phone. She was studying the screen, her fingers flying, when a sharp tug almost pulled her off her feet.

Instinct rather than good sense made her grip tighten around the holdall slung over her shoulder. The tussle was short but the thief who grunted and swore at length at her had size on his side; although he was skinny, he was wiry and tall and he easily escaped with her bag.

'Help... Thief!'

Dozens must have heard her anguished cry but nobody reacted until the tall hooded youth—a stereotype if there ever was one—who was shouldering his way through the crowd clutching her bag hit one pedestrian who did not move aside.

She saw the thief bounce off this immovable object and hit the pavement face down before crowds hid him and her bag from view.

She missed the thief shaking his head as he looked up, a snarl on his thin, acne-marked face aimed at the man at whose feet he lay sprawled. The snarl melted abruptly and was replaced by a flash of fear as he released the bag handle as though it were alight and, lurching to his feet, ran away.

Draco sighed. If he weren't already very late he might have chased the culprit but he was, so instead he bent to pick up the stolen bag, which immediately opened, disgorging its contents at his feet and all over the pavement.

Draco blinked. In his thirty-three years he'd seen a lot and few things had the power to surprise him any more. In fact, only that very morning he'd asked himself if he was in a rut—the trouble with ruts was you didn't always recognise you were in one—but standing ankle-deep in ladies' underwear—wildly sexy lingerie, to be precise—most definitely surprised him.

Now that, he thought, was something that didn't happen every day of the week—at least not to him.

One dark mobile brow elevated, and with a half-smile tugging his sensually sculpted lips upwards he bent forward and hooked a bra from the top of the silky heap. Silk, and a shocking-pink tartan, it was definitely a statement and, if he was any judge, a D cup.

Under his breath he read the hand-sewn label along one seam.

'Eve's Temptation.' It was catchy and the name rang a faint bell.

Had Rachel had something similar in a more subdued colour? He sighed. While he missed the great sex, if he was honest—and he generally was—he didn't miss Rachel herself, and he had no regrets about his decision to terminate their short and, he had assumed, mutually satisfactory arrangement.

Only she had crossed the line. It had started with the 'we' and 'us' comments—*we* could stop off at my parents', my sister has offered *us* her ski lodge as it'll be empty at New Year. Draco blamed himself for allowing it to pass as long as he had, but in his defence the sex had been very good indeed.

Things had finally come to a head a couple of months ago when she had *accidentally* bumped into him in the middle of an exclusive department store on one of the rare occasions when he was able to spend some quality time with his daughter.

It wasn't her appallingly obvious efforts to ingratiate herself with Josie that had stuck in Draco's mind; it was his daughter's comment on the way home.

'Don't be too brutal will you, Dad, when you dump her?'

The worried expression in her eyes had made him realise that he'd become complacent, he'd allowed the once clearly defined lines between his home life and the other aspects of his life to blur. It was more important to keep that protective wall around his home life now that Josie was getting older than it ever had been.

The day he had looked at his baby and realised that her mother wasn't coming back he had sworn that this desertion would not affect her; he would protect her, give her security. He had made some inevitable mistakes along the way but at least he hadn't allowed her to form attachments with the women he had enjoyed fleeting liaisons with over the years and risk being hurt when they too left.

'Nice,' he murmured, running his thumb over the fine butter-soft silk.

'That's mine.' Eve's determined gaze was fixed on the pink tartan bra that she hoped was going to be next season's best-seller.

'You're Eve?'

'Yes.' The response was automatic. She could, if she'd wanted, have claimed ownership of, not just the name, but the bra and the brand of which she was justifiably proud, though there was a strong possibility that, as on numerous previous occasions, the information would be received with scepticism.

She understood why: it was all about appearances and she simply didn't look the part of a successful businesswoman, let alone one who was the founder of a successful underwear company that had based its brand on glamour with a quirky edge that not only looked good but was comfortable to wear.

'It was very brave of you to stop that thief running away with my bag. I hope he didn't hurt you.' Her smile faded dramatically as she looked up into the face of the man who was holding her sample. 'I'm very...' She cleared her throat and swallowed, her tongue uncomfortably glued to the roof of her mouth.

There were several other equally disturbing accompanying symptoms, and it was so totally unexpected that it took her a few heart-racing moments to put a name to the frantic heart-pounding, uncontrolled heat rush and visceral clutch that dug into her stomach and tightened like a fist. Even the fine invisible hair on her forearms was tingling in response to what this man exuded, which was—give it a name, Evie, and move on, she told herself sternly—raw sex!

Either that or this was a much less publicised symptom of jet lag!

'Grateful.' For small mercies—I didn't drool, she added silently, refusing to contemplate the mortifying possibility that she had been standing there with her mouth open for more than a few seconds.

Now that she was able to study his face with the objectivity she prided herself on, Eve could see that, though her first impressions were right—he was quite remarkably good–looking; maybe the most good-looking man she'd ever seen up close—it wasn't his face or athletic body that had caused her nervous system to go into meltdown, it was the aura of raw sexuality that he exuded like a force field.

That made sense, because obvious good looks didn't do it for her—they never had—and his were very, *very* obvious! It wasn't that she had anything against cheekbones you could cut yourself on, classic square firm jawlines, overtly sensual lips or eyelashes that long—actually the crazily long and spiky eyelashes framing deep-set liquid dark eyes were kind of nice—it was just that Eve had always liked a face with character belonging to men who spent less time looking in the mirror than she did. And of course being a *man* he didn't have to worry about the thin white scar beside his mouth. It didn't matter that the likelihood was he'd done it doing something as mundane as falling off his bike as a kid; it added to the air of brooding danger and mystery he exuded.

The thought of being considered a hero for just standing still and letting the thief bump into him drew an ironic smile. 'I'll survive.'

Well, his ego would at least—it could obviously withstand a force-ten gale. The uncharacteristically uncharitable thought brought a furrow to her brow but for some reason just looking at him made her skin prickle with antagonism.

Draco gave up the D cup and studied the claimant, a breathless pink-faced female who snatched it from his fingers. The bra couldn't be hers as she was definitely not a D cup. Actually, he was pretty sure she was not wearing a bra at all, and there was a definite chill in the air—well, this was London; when wasn't there? His interested glance drifted and lingered on her small but pert breasts heaving dramatically beneath the loose white shirt she wore.

Eve, catching the direction of his stare, felt her colour deepen even though she knew she was being a bit paranoid. Nothing could be less revealing than her shirt; anything tighter rubbed the small scar below her shoulder blade that was still a little tender.

'Thank you.' She struggled to inject some warmth into her response and, just to be on the safe side, fastened her jacket, taking care not to put too much pressure on her shoulder. By next week it ought to be healed enough for her to be able to wear a bra again.

'You're actually called Eve?' His curious gaze roamed over her heart-shaped face. If the original Eve had possessed a mouth that lush and inviting he for one would have cut Adam some slack.

'Let me guess—you're Adam.' She sighed as though it was a tired line she'd heard often.

'No, I'm Draco, but you can call me Adam if you want to.'

'A lovely offer but I doubt we'll ever be on first-name terms.' She thanked him again, crammed the last camisole into the bag and snapped it closed then, after tilting a nod in his direction, hurried away.

He's not watching, Eve, so why the hip swaying? she berated herself crossly.

He was watching.

* * *

Frazer Campbell, a meticulous man, reached the bottom of the page, readjusted his half-moon specs and began at the top of the page again. Draco's jaw clenched as he struggled to control his impatience.

'I am assuming this is an empty threat?' he asked.

The letter, though sprinkled with pseudo-legal phrases, was written by hand, the writing his ex-wife's, the wording definitely not... Draco strongly suspected that she had received some help with it, and even without the headed notepaper it didn't take a genius to figure out who from. His ex-wife's fiancé, Edward Weston, had got his seat in Parliament on the family value ticket—so it wasn't hard to see where he was coming from. Selling yourself to the British public as a defender of family values was tough when your future bride had played a very peripheral role in her own daughter's life.

Draco didn't personally know the man, though he'd heard him called a joke on more than one occasion and maybe, if the subject he had chosen to poke his nose into had been any other, he might have been laughing—but he wasn't.

One thing he absolutely did not joke about was his daughter's welfare.

Frazer, older by several years than the man who was pacing the room restless as a caged panther in the enclosed space, smoothed the paper with the flat of his hand as he laid it back on his desk—it had landed there in an angry, crumpled ball.

'It's not really a threat as such, is it?' Edward Weston came across as pompous but he wasn't a total idiot and anyone who threatened Draco would have to be; the wealthy London-based Italian entrepreneur was famous for many things but turning the other cheek was not one of them! Frazer counted himself lucky to call Draco friend—you tended to bond pretty quickly with someone you got buried in an avalanche with—but if he hadn't been, Draco's reputation alone would have made him someone Frazer would have avoided.

The comment earned him a flash from Draco's dark eyes.

'Do you want to hear what I think or what you want to hear?' Frazer's shaggy brows twitched into a straight line as he noticed for the first time

what his friend was wearing: full morning suit.
'Your wedding?' he asked cautiously.

'Marriage!' The single word made the speaker's
opinion of that institution quite clear, it dripped
with such acid scorn.

'Shame—if you were married it would be a perfect solution to the problem. There would be no
question of your daughter not having...' he paused
to consult the letter and read out loud '..."a stable female influence in her life".' Frazer smiled
at his own joke while Draco, his dark eyes glint-
ing not with laughter but with cynicism, lowered
his long, lean frame into a chair on the opposite
side of the desk.

'I'd sooner move my mother in.' The other man
laughed; he had met Veronica Morelli. 'You make
a mistake,' Draco continued, 'and you don't repeat
it, unless of course you're a total fool.'

Frazer, who was blissfully happy in his second
marriage, did not take offence. 'Do you think it's
safe to come to a fool for expensive legal advice?'

Draco gave a tight grin that deepened the lines
radiating from his deep-set eyes and briefly lent
warmth and humour to the dark depths. 'There
are exceptions to every rule,' he conceded. 'And

I'm coming to you as a trusted friend—I couldn't afford what you charge.'

The older man snorted. Draco Morelli had been born to wealth and privilege, he could have sat back and enjoyed what he had inherited, but he was a natural entrepreneur and to his Italian family's occasional bemusement over the last ten years he had made a series of financial investments that had made his name a byword for success in financial circles.

Under his smile was iron resolve. Draco's short-lived marriage had been by anyone's standards a total disaster but it had given him the daughter he adored so he could never regret it—but to deliberately take that route again...?

It was not going to happen.

He had affairs, just not *love* affairs. He did not dress things up and recognised that for him sex was simply a basic need; he had proved over and over again that the emotional element was not necessary. It required no effort on his part to maintain an emotional buffer—there were even occasions when he did not much like the women who shared his bed. What did require some effort on his part was keeping his daughter, now a scarily mature and impressively grounded thirteen, as ignorant as possible of his affairs.

'She's talking custody rights or at least Edward is.' His ex's latest was a very unlikely choice for a woman who normally went for men considerably her junior. It was hard to think of a more unlikely couple and Draco doubted it would last despite the ostentatious rock on Clare's finger, but if he was wrong—well, good luck to them.

But he wasn't going to allow his daughter to have her life thrown into turmoil because Clare had discovered her inner earth mother—not on his watch!

'I am fond of Clare—let's face it, it's hard not to be fond of Clare,' her ex-husband conceded. 'But I wouldn't trust her to take care of a cat, let alone a teenager. Can you imagine it…?' He shook his dark head, grimacing at the mental image.

When they handed out the responsibility gene Clare was out of the room. Josie had been three months old when his ex had gone out for a facial and manicure and not come back. Left effectively a single parent at twenty, Draco had had to learn some new skills very quickly—he still was learning.

Fatherhood was a constant challenge, as was resisting his mother's interference. When he'd told the grieving widow that she needed a new challenge in her life, he certainly hadn't intended that challenge to be him! When Veronica Morelli wasn't turning up on his doorstep without warning with large suitcases she was trying to set him up with suitable women—the marrying kind.

'She's asking for joint custody, Draco, and she is the girl's mother.' Frazer held up a hand to stem the eruption his comment invited and continued calmly. 'But, no, given the circumstances and her history I don't think there is any prospect of any court coming down on her side, even if it got that far and she did marry Edward Weston. It's not as if she doesn't have access, very reasonable access, already to Josie.'

Draco nodded. No matter what her faults were, his ex-wife was Josie's mother and she was in her own way fond of her only child. Clare's *fondness* meant months could go by and their daughter would have no contact beyond the occasional text or email from her mother, then she would appear loaded with gifts and was for a time a doting mother, until something else caught her interest.

Draco's objectivity when he thought of his ex-wife was still tinged with cynicism but the corrosive anger had long since gone. He was even able to recognise that it had always been aimed more at himself than Clare, and with some justification when you considered the stubborn sentimentalism masquerading as love that had made him go through with a marriage that had had impending disaster written all over it.

'So you don't think I have anything to worry about?' he asked.

'I'm a lawyer, Draco—in my world there is always something to worry about.'

'Sure, I might walk under a bus.' He glanced at his watch and got to his feet, brushing an invisible speck from the perfectly tailored pale grey jacket. Actually, he was catching a helicopter rather than a bus to the wedding of Charlie Latimer; he found weddings depressing, and boring, but Josie was very excited about dressing up and he was making an effort for her sake.

'Is it true that Latimer is marrying his cook?'

'I haven't a clue.' Draco, who had less liking for gossip than he did weddings, replied honestly while he thought of a pink tartan bra and a pair of big green eyes...

On his way down in the elevator he thought some more about the bra's owner, and he was so involved in the mental images that there was a twenty-second delay before he noticed that the lift door had opened.

Focus, Draco... He did not for a second doubt his ability to do just that; it was a case of prioritising and he was good at that. It had been this ability that had got him past the first few weeks and months after Clare had walked out. He could have carried on being bitter, twisted and generally wallowing in a morass of self-pity; he could have allowed himself to be defined by that failure.

But he hadn't.

After that reminder, keeping his libido on a leash was relatively simple and he told himself that Green Eyes was definitely not his type. Still, there had been *something* about her...

'Oh, I'm so sorry.'

Draco placed a steadying hand on the arm of the young woman who had not so accidentally collided with him. Blonde and stunning, she *was* his type.

His smile was automatic and lacking a spontaneity that the recipient appeared not to notice. Standing on one foot, she had grabbed his arm for support. 'Are you all right?' he asked.

'I wasn't looking where I was going. It's these heels.'

She rotated one shapely ankle, inviting him to look, and Draco, being polite, did.

'I don't know if you remember…?' The eyelashes did some overtime and the pout was good but he'd seen better, he mused. Now, if Green Eyes ever decided to pout, those lips would have given her a natural advantage. 'But we met at the charity gala last month.'

'Of course,' Draco lied. There had been many attractive women there and good manners plus boredom meant he had probably flirted with a few. 'If you'll excuse me, I'm pushed for time—' His grimace was a product of impatience but the recipient chose to interpret it as regret.

'Shame, but you've got my number and I'd love to take you up on that offer of dinner.' Before Draco could even pretend to recall any such offer, let alone extend or retract it, the blonde suddenly stopped, her eyes widening at him as she waved her hand wildly at a figure about to cross the road.

'Eve!' she shrieked, forgetting the sexy purr.

Eve heaved a sigh and, pasting a smile on her face, turned without enthusiasm.

She had spotted them fifty yards back, hardly surprising as the couple who were standing at the entrance to the underground car park where she had left her car were drawing attention the way only *beautiful* people did. Eve had nothing a*gainst* beautiful people in general—her best friend was one, after all. She didn't even envy them their head-turning good looks because being the focus of attention everywhere you went was the stuff her nightmares were made of. It was just that this man…talk about bad luck…and talk about a *stereotype*!

It had been no shock to see him with the blonde—just a massive shock to bump into him again. As status symbols went, an underwear model on your arm was right up there with a big flash fuel-guzzling car, for alpha men like her father. But, to be perfectly fair, this man *wasn't* her father and she was making judgements like this *because*…?

Because of the liquid ache low in her pelvis, because a man who had barely brushed her life had finally given her the faintest *inkling* of the sort of irrational attraction that her own mother must have experienced in order to make her forget the principles she had instilled in her own daughter and have an affair with a married man.

Keep it in proportion, Eve. It's been a tough week and it isn't over yet, she reminded herself as she averted her gaze from the long scarlet nails that were possessively stroking his sleeve.

Her heart was thudding so hard that she could hardly hear her response to the woman almost as famous for her rich and famous boyfriends as she was for her perfect body. If he was Sabrina's latest that made him rich…well, that explained the arrogant air of smug assurance that really got under her skin and, as for famous, well…these days who wasn't? Even she could type her name into a search engine and have pages appear.

'Hello, Sabrina.' She acknowledged the tall stranger from earlier with an unsmiling nod while she struggled against the effects of his brain-mushing charisma.

'Eve, it's so good to see you.' Eve got a whiff of

heavy perfume as the air either side of her face was kissed. 'And perfect timing too. I can tell you in person…' The dramatic pause stretched a little too long before her announcement. 'I'm available.'

Eve always hated the feeling of walking into a conversation halfway through. Was she meant to know what the woman was talking about…?

Draco watched the expression on Eve's face; it was clear she didn't have a clue what the blonde was talking about. He fought a laugh with more success than he had fought the gut kick of lust he had no defence against when he had recognised the petite figure who, unless he was mistaken, had been about to make good an escape.

Draco wasn't used to women who crossed the road to avoid him—they did the reverse occasionally—and he wondered what he'd done to make her look down her elegant little nose at him. His ego remained intact—it was pretty robust most of the time—but his interest was piqued. What would it take to melt that stern disapproval into uncritical adoration? He was setting his sights too high, he realised; he didn't want adoration from her, just a smile. Although adoration might be nice after a long night getting to know her better…?

'You are?' Eve asked Sabrina.

'Yes, but my agent said he is *still* waiting for a
call back from your office about the new campaign...so-o-o exciting. He said something about
you not using models this time.' She rolled her
eyes. 'But I told him it's obvious you think I'm
still committed to the supermarket people, but
the thing is I decided to call it a day with them as
they were just going so *down market* and not the
sort of thing I want to be associated with at all.'

'Sorry, Sabrina, but I've been out of the country
so the agency has been doing all the recruiting.'

'But you'll have the final say...right?'

Eve was tempted to say she'd be in touch but her
innate sense of honesty won out. It would be unfair to string the other girl along. 'Actually your
agent had it right; we're not using models, just
real women...not that you're not real, but you're
not ordinary. What I mean is—'

'She means, Sabrina, that normal women can
never aspire to looking like you do.'

Had anyone else made the intervention Eve
might have felt grateful, but instead she found
herself biting back a childish retort of *Don't tell
me what I mean.*

'You're so sweet.' Sabrina pressed a soft kiss on his lean cheek.

Eve rolled her eyes and thought *perleeze* just as, above the model's head, the dark eyes found her own. His sleek ebony brows lifted and he smiled, the sort of smile that she imagined a fox might produce when contemplating a defenceless chick.

Eve narrowed her eyes and lifted her chin in silent challenge. She was not defenceless or stupid enough to smile at a man who could flirt with one woman while another was kissing him!

As she pulled away the model's complacent expression faded. 'But isn't that the idea? They all think if they buy the product they will look like me,' she said, looking confused.

Eve heaved a sigh. She had neither the time nor the inclination to explain herself to this woman whom she ungenerously stigmatised as totally self-centred. Her eyes slid of their own volition to her tall, arrogant companion…not a case of opposites attracting in their case, she decided waspishly, but like meeting like. 'Sorry, but I must run…lovely to bump into you…' She could hear the insincerity in her voice but didn't hang around to see if anyone else had. Head down, she headed for the entrance to the underground car park.

The brief encounter had left her feeling... She laughed, the sound echoing around the concrete shell, and shook her head. If there was ever a moment when she was allowed to feel weird it was today! Ignoring the fact her hand was still shaking, she fished her key ring out of her bag.

She had enough to deal with today without analysing the skin-tingling effect of a sexy stranger who represented pretty much everything she despised in a man. She was jet-lagged, facing the prospect of biting her tongue while her mother threw away her life and freedom and—she rubbed her shoulder and grimaced—she'd just had minor surgery. She was definitely permitted a little *weird*.

'I'm curious, why do you keep running away from me?'

Eve started violently, nearly losing her grip on her keys as she spun around. How on earth could someone that big make so little sound? He was standing a few feet away just beyond a sleek gleaming monster that was the motoring equivalent of him. If she cared about cars she would probably know what it was, but she didn't so in her head she simply grouped it under the heading of *look at me I have loads of money.*

She lifted her chin. 'There are laws against stalking.' She knew perfectly well that none of the adrenaline pumping through her body was the result of fear…which was too worrying to think about just now.

'And quite right too; speaking from experience it can be—'

Her hoot of derision cut him off. 'God, it must be so tough being irresistible to the opposite sex.' She only just stopped herself hastily adding she was not one of that number, but then actions always spoke louder than words and she hoped she was channelling contempt and not lust. There was no way in the world that he could know about the shameful heat at the juncture of her thighs.

'I'm flattered—'

'Not my intention.' She sounded breathless, and she definitely felt breathless as she fought to hold onto her defiance in the face of the suggestion of a smile her retort had produced.

She didn't know him.

She disliked him.

She had never felt such a strong reaction to a man. Ever.

'Relax, *cara*, this is my car.' He pressed his key fob and the monster's lights flashed.

Calling herself every kind of a fool—sure, you're so irresistible every drop-dead gorgeous man has to follow you, she thought scathingly— she wrenched her own car door open.

'Would you like dinner sometime?'

Draco was almost as surprised to hear himself make the offer as she looked to hear it. It had been an uncharacteristic impulse kicked into life by the sight of her getting in that car and the knowledge he would never see her again.

'Well, it seems like such a waste…all this…' his long fingers moved in an expressive gesture that encompassed the space between them '…chem- istry.'

Draco felt satisfied with this explanation for his uncharacteristically impulsive behaviour. She looked—he studied the small heart-shaped face lifted to him—less so.

The soft flush that covered her skin and the angry sparkle in her luminous green eyes made him tip his head in a nod of approval. There was passion there. He knew he'd been right about the chemistry.

'I'm assuming it's an ego thing with you...you have to have every woman your willing slave.'

He adopted a thoughtful expression as though considering the charge, then slowly shook his head. 'Slave suggests passive,' he purred, staring at her mouth with an expression that made her stomach quiver with a mixture of anger and lust she refused to acknowledge. 'I find passive boring.'

'Well, I find men who have massive egos boring!' she jeered, and slid onto the driver's seat. 'And there is no chemistry,' she yelled, before slamming the car door.

She could hear the sound of his low throaty laughter above the metallic scream as she crunched the gears before finding reverse.

CHAPTER TWO

THE TWO YOUNG women who stood waiting in the bedroom were both in their mid-twenties but there the similarity ended.

The girl who sat on the edge of the four-poster, one slim ankle crossed over the other, was an elegant, tall, blue-eyed blonde. The other one, who had spent the last five minutes prowling restlessly up and down the room, her heels making angry tapping sounds on the age-darkened polished boards, was neither tall nor blonde, and, even though the two women were dressed identically, she was somehow not elegant.

She was five three without heels and had chestnut-brown hair. Making no concession to the occasion—the dress was enough—she wore it as she always did: scraped into the heavy knot on her slender neck. It was not a style statement, though it did reveal the length of her neck and the delicate angle of her rounded jaw, just convenient. When exposed to even a sniff of moisture it fell into a mass of uncontrollable kinky waves and Eve liked control in all aspects of her life.

There had been a period when she had struggled to emulate her friend Hannah's effortless elegance, but no matter how hard she tried it just didn't happen. She always ended up looking as though she were dressing up in her mother's clothes. Gradually Eve had found her own style or—as an exasperated Hannah put it—*uniform*, which was a little unfair. Not all Eve's trouser suits were black—some were navy—and who had time to shop anyhow when they had a business to run? You couldn't afford to relax in this competitive world.

'Ouch!' She tripped over the skirt of her duckegg-blue silk bridesmaid dress and banged her knee on the window seat. The pain made her green eyes film with tears.

'Well, if you'd come to a fitting it wouldn't be too long.' Harriet gave an affectionate smile and shook her head. The frantic last-minute pinning meant that Eve's dress had a sort of waist but the neckline of the fitted bodice still had a tendency to gape and slip down a couple of inches if Eve moved too quickly—and Eve moved quickly a lot. Her friend was never still mentally or physically, and just watching her made Hannah feel tired.

Eve gave another hitch accompanied by a hiss of exasperation. If she'd been more naturally blessed in the boob department it wouldn't be a problem, but even with the tissues tucked into the strapless bra that was chafing the partially healed scar on her shoulder blade she was one cup size short of keeping the bodice up.

On the plus side, while she was focusing on not exposing herself she wasn't thinking about her mother throwing herself away on a man who didn't deserve her! The furrow in danger of becoming permanent in her wide brow deepened because, impending wardrobe malfunction or not, she was thinking about it and had been ever since her mother had rung excited as a schoolgirl with the glad tidings. A week was not a long time but Eve had prayed her mother would come to her senses.

She hadn't.

'The measurements you sent must have been way off. Sarah said you've lost weight since she saw you last,' Hannah commented.

Eve felt a stab of guilt that intensified when Hannah made excuses for her.

'I know Australia is a long way to come for a fitting.'

'I didn't go there to avoid my mother!' Eve protested.

'I never thought you did.'

Until now, thought Eve, wishing she could keep her big mouth shut. 'I don't see what all the big hurry is for anyhow.' The way Hannah was looking at her made Eve frown. 'Well, do you?'

Hannah pressed a protective hand to her stomach, reflecting on how odd it was that Eve, who was super smart and intuitive in so many ways, could not have at least *suspected*. She had often felt a little intimidated by her friend's quick brain and focused drive, but for all her ability there were times when Eve couldn't see what was right under her nose and this was one of those occasions. Hannah swiftly changed the subject; now was probably not the time to voice her suspicions.

'Well, you made it back in time, which is the main thing. I'd have loved you to be at my wedding too,' Hannah added wistfully.

'I didn't get an invite.'

'I barely made it there myself.'

'Fine, be mysterious,' Eve grumbled, thinking that whatever the full story behind her friend's marriage to the Prince of Surana she had never seen Hannah looking happier or more beautiful— she was positively glowing.

'But you must be happy, Evie; this is what we have always wanted. For us to finally be a family.'

Eve swallowed the retort on the tip of her tongue.

She could hardly say to the man's daughter your dad is a sad loser and I never wanted him to marry my mum. I wanted her to wake up to the fact he was using her and end the sordid, secret affair.

She had no idea what had happened to make Charles Latimer, not only acknowledge the long-term affair with his cook after years of hiding it, but propose to her and then invite half the world to the wedding. She glanced out of the window at the sound of another helicopter coming in to land—another VIP, she thought sourly. Charles Latimer certainly moved in glittering circles.

Her jaw set as she turned away. 'What's keeping her?' As far as Eve was concerned it was a disaster!

When the silence stretched Hannah's expression grew anxious. 'It's very romantic.'

Eve's brows lifted. 'You think?'

'You know, I agree with you totally that Dad has behaved very selfishly over the years to Sarah, but your mum is the best thing that has happened to him,' Hannah said earnestly. 'I'm just glad he's woken up to it. I can't wait for Sarah to be my mum.'

'She's a good mum to have,' Eve said, a lump forming in her throat as she thought of all the sacrifices her single mum had made over the years. She deserved the best and she was getting Charlie Latimer. Eve's small hands tightened into fists, her nails inscribing half-moons into her palms. 'I think she already thinks of you as a daughter.'

'I hope so.' Hannah's blue eyes filled with emotional tears, which she blinked to clear as the door to the interconnecting room opened to reveal the bride.

Her face almost as white as the dress she was wearing, Sarah Curtis stood for a moment framed in the doorway before taking a step and almost immediately grabbing onto a table to steady herself. Reacting faster than Eve, Hannah was on her feet in an instant, her beautiful face creased in lines of concern as she rushed to supply a steadying hand to the older woman.

'Are you all right, Sarah?'

Eve blinked. She wasn't seeing her mother's pale face as she was transfixed by the miles and miles of tulle her mother was wearing. The first sight of the outfit on its hanger earlier had rendered her literally speechless and it had been left to Hannah to make the necessary congratulatory noises. Somehow she had managed to sound totally sincere.

Hannah had to be a better actress than she had previously thought because the get-up was quite memorably awful and—what was worse—*inappropriate*. Eve didn't know what had possessed her mother to suddenly decide to channel her inner princess!

Sarah gave a wan smile. 'All I need is a bit of blusher.'

Hannah threw her a knowing look, her hands on her hips, and the older woman sighed heavily, suddenly looking sheepish. 'All right, I wasn't planning to tell you girls till later because I'm not quite twelve weeks yet and—'

It had to weigh a ton, Eve thought, sizing up the intricate beading on the mile-long train that was many a girl's dream. But not hers; she had never dreamed of wearing such an elaborate get-up. Did that make her weird? If so she was glad, she decided defiantly! How did a woman in her forties think that it was in any way appropriate to wear a white meringue wedding dress?

She dragged her gaze upwards just as Hannah, looking totally regal in her beautifully fitting dress—actually she was a princess for real these days, a fact that Eve still hadn't got her head around—walked over and hugged her mother. Both women were crying, to Eve's confusion. Had her mum finally realised that the dress was a disaster?

'You could always ditch the train,' Eve suggested, trying to remain practical and upbeat for her mother's sake. She knew she just had to suck it up today and be there for her mum in the future when things went sour with Charles, as they inevitably would.

Sarah, sniffing, laughed. 'I wish it were that simple. I didn't have any morning sickness at all with you, darling, but this time...' She rolled her eyes and accepted the glass of water that Hannah passed her.

Playing mental catch–up, Eve blinked. *Morning sickness*…? She must have misheard. You only got morning sickness when you were…*pregnant*!

A stunned vacant expression clouding her green eyes, she felt herself hit a mental brick wall. The impact made her mind go blank and she sat down with a gentle thud on the window seat. Paler even than her mother, she sat there not even breathing until finally her chest lifted in a long shuddering sigh and her lashes swept down in a concealing curtain. She stared at her hands and waited for the dull metronome thud in her ears to subside, but it didn't.

'There, that's better—all you needed was a bit of colour.'

A hand absently rubbing the nape of her neck, Eve looked up as her friend applied a finishing flick of blusher to the older woman's cheeks.

'You're p-pregnant, Mum. H-how?' Two sets of raised eyebrows turned her way and Eve blushed. She was regressing; she no longer stuttered or blushed. 'Well, I suppose that explains it.'

'Explains what, Eve?' Sarah asked.

Eve shook her head and thought why the rich scumbag Charlie Latimer had suddenly decided, not only to make his secret affair with his cook public knowledge, but to marry the woman who had been his mistress. It didn't involve a sudden attack of respect or love for Sarah; it was all about the possibility of an heir.

Not that Hannah looked as though she minded the possibility of being disinherited—her friend looked delighted.

'I knew it,' Hannah said smugly as she dabbed the moisture from around her soon-to-be step-mother's eyes. 'Whoever invented waterproof mascara deserves a medal—not that you'd know about that, Eve.' She flashed her friend, who had been blessed with naturally thick dark lashes that required no embellishment, an envious smile before turning back to Sarah. 'I said to Kamel last night that I thought you might be but he said that just because I'm—' She stopped and covered her mouth with her hand. 'I wasn't meant to say anything until Kamel has told his uncle because of all this protocol. You won't breathe a word, will you…?'

'Oh, Hannah, darling, Kamel must be thrilled!'

Sarah's waterproof mascara was once again being put to the test as she reached up to hug Hannah.

'We both are, but Kamel is acting as though I'm made of glass. He won't let me do a thing, and the man is driving me crazy,' Hannah confided with a laugh.

The expression in her friend's eyes when she said her husband's name made Eve look away feeling uncomfortable, almost as though she had intruded. Eve was prepared to like the prince her friend had married because he was clearly as potty about Hannah as she was about him, but the cynic in her wondered how long the honeymoon period would last.

'You're both having babies.' Eve was still playing mental catch-up.

Looking mistily ecstatic, Sarah clapped her hands. 'Isn't that incredible? Our family is growing, girls.'

'A real family,' Hannah chimed in.

Eve cleared her throat. It was obviously her turn to respond, but what to say…? She managed a faint and unimaginative, *'Incredible.'*

She'd moved a long way on since she had lain awake at night wishing she had a *real* family. Eve had pretty quickly realised that not having a father, at least not one willing to acknowledge she existed, was actually a blessing, not a curse. Unlike the majority of her classmates she had been spared the trauma of seeing her parents going through an ugly divorce or separation.

Her mum had not even had boyfriends until she came to work for Hannah's father. Hannah had caught on much sooner than Eve and she had been more concerned by the secrecy than the relationship itself.

For Eve, it hadn't just been the secrecy, it had been everything, and the longer the affair had lasted, the deeper her anger had grown as she'd watched helpless to do anything while her mother allowed history to repeat itself as she had become what amounted to the plaything of man who treated her like the hired help in front of his rich and powerful friends.

Charles Latimer might not be married but in every other way he was her own father—a selfish loser who used and humiliated her mum. Of course, back then Sarah had been a young impressionable student on her first holiday job—easy pickings for her unscrupulous rich employer.

What Eve could not understand was how her mother could let it happen again when she was now an independent, intelligent woman. How could she allow herself to be used and humiliated like this…? Where were her pride and self-respect?

Did Mum realise that he was only marrying her because of the baby? Eve wondered. Well, at least he was one step up the evolutionary scale of slime from her own father, whose contribution when he had learnt of her had been to write a signed note that included the words *get rid of it*.

Eve had never told her mum she had found the note while searching for her birth certificate, and she'd never let on she knew the identity of her father. Instead she had carefully folded it and put it back in the box that held her birth certificate.

'Having a baby at your age…' She sensed rather than saw Hannah's look of warning. 'Not that you're old, obviously.'

Her mother managed a wan smile at the retrieval. 'Always the soul of tact, Evie.'

Eve watched as Hannah and her mum exchanged a look. She didn't resent the rapport that her mum and her friend had but, though she rarely acknowledged it, there were occasions when she did envy it. Eve was her daughter but Hannah was a kindred spirit.

'I just meant…' She paused and thought, What did you mean? 'Couldn't it be dangerous…for you, and the baby?' But not for Charlie Latimer. Eve felt the anger and resentment she had always felt towards the man deepen so that they lay like an icy block behind her breastbone.

'Loads of women in their forties have babies these days, Evie.' Hannah proceeded to tick off a list of well-known celebrities Sarah's age and older who had given birth recently.

'And I'll have a lot more support than I did last time around; your father has been marvellous, Hannah.'

Too little too late, Eve thought, before the guilt kicked in; it always did when she thought about all the things her mum had given up to be a single parent. She finally deserved some happiness but was she likely to find it with Charlie Latimer…?

Eve clenched her jaw. No, her mum deserved more—she deserved better after all the sacrifices she had made.

Wanting to give her mum the things she deserved had been behind Eve's choice to reject the prestigious university scholarship she'd been offered and instead start her own firm. It hadn't been easy. All the banks had turned the inexperienced eighteen-year-old away and in the end it had been a charitable trust set up to promote youth enterprise that had been convinced by her business plan and the rest, as they said, was history. Nowadays she was held up as one of the trust's success stories, and regularly mentored young aspiring entrepreneurs and helped raise funds.

It had been a year ago that Eve had been able to go to her mother and triumphantly tell her she didn't need to work for Charles Latimer, and that she, Eve, was able to support her while she did what she wanted: a university course, open her own restaurant…anything.

Good plan with one problem. It turned out her mum was already doing what she wanted: she wanted to waste her talents, to slave away for a man like Charles Latimer. Eve had been angry, hurt and frustrated. She knew that a distance had formed between them since that day. She had let it form.

Sarah's green eyes filled again as she scanned

her daughter's face and asked anxiously, 'You're all right with this, aren't you, Eve?'

'I'm really happy for you, Mum,' she said quietly, thinking, If that man hurts you I'll make him wish he had never been born.

Maybe she was a better actress than she thought, or maybe her mum just wanted to believe the lie, but either way Sarah visibly relaxed.

CHAPTER THREE

THOUGH THE LAWN had been rigged out with a positive village of canvas to house the reception, the ceremony itself was being held in the timbered great hall of Brent Manor, Charles's country estate. The guests, entertained by a string quartet, were seated in semi-circular rows around a central aisle and the dramatic staircase was lit up to give everyone a good view of the bridal party as they made their big entrance.

The warm-up act was followed by a well-known soprano, who belted out a couple of numbers that reduced some people to tears. For Draco it felt like a visit to the cinema when the trailers went on for so long you forgot what you'd actually come to see.

Finally the wedding march started, but his sigh of relief earned him a poke in the ribs from his daughter, so he dutifully turned his head to watch the slow progression of the wedding party down the staircase. His interest was initially directed towards the tall bridesmaid who was the new wife of his friend Kamel.

Draco studied her as she walked past the row where he sat. Beautiful, he thought as his attention drifted for a moment to the second bridesmaid, who up to this point had been blocked from his view by the statuesque blonde.

He experienced a jolt of shock closely followed by an even stronger jolt of lust as he identified the slender creature as this morning's green-eyed Eve! While he did not believe in fate or karma or even coincidence, Draco did believe in not wasting opportunities.

She made Draco think of the Degas he had purchased several years ago: the big-eyed delicate-featured dancer in it possessed the same ethereal quality. Not that there was anything balletic about this woman's hunched shoulders and the expression in her wide-spaced eyes was less dreamy and more abject misery. As his glance lingered he realised that there was nothing joyous in any aspect of her body language, including the smile painted onto her face.

As she drew level with him he could almost

feel the tension rolling off her in waves. In the hollow at the base of her white throat—she had quite beautiful collarbones, he mused—a pulse throbbed. It wasn't just tension rolling off her, he realised; it was a level of misery you would have expected to see at a funeral, not a wedding!

At the precise moment she drew level with him Draco got a glimpse of something else you didn't expect to see at a wedding! It happened so quickly that if he hadn't been staring at her he'd have missed it, and she handled the dilemma rather well. Without skipping a beat or looking to left or right she grabbed the bodice of her dress before it slithered all the way down to her waist so it was a bit of a blur, but he got a glimpse of a white lacy strapless bra through which he saw the faint pink outline of nipples and a birthmark shaped like a moon high on the left side of her ribcage.

As the service went on he found himself staring, not at the bride and groom, but at Eve... Was that really her name or a marketing tool? He was curious about her misery but a lot more interested in seeing that birthmark again... The white lace was pretty but in his head she was wearing pink tartan silk. He had felt instant attractions to women before but never one as consuming as that he felt when he looked at this woman.

His eyes didn't leave her all the way through the ceremony. Then, as the procession led by the jubilant happy couple returned down the aisle, she was briefly hidden from sight by the bride and groom. Draco, who had struggled to leave his cynicism behind, had time to think, I give them a couple of months, before he saw her come into view once more. Unlike the new Princess of Surana, who was smiling at every familiar face she saw, his bridesmaid was staring fixedly ahead. She radiated a sultry sexiness that he could almost taste.

She had actually walked right past him, when she suddenly turned her head. Their collision of eyes had such an impact that for a split second he stopped breathing and she stopped walking. The air whistled through his flared nostrils as he exhaled slowly, and watched the colour wash over her skin.

His wink brought a flash of anger to her dark-framed emerald eyes but did not lessen the tension in the muscles around his mouth and eyes… The hunger he was feeling was no laughing matter.

* * *

Once she'd accepted it was really happening, Eve just wanted it to be over. For the most part she managed to blank out the actual ceremony. There had been that wardrobe malfunction but she was pretty confident that no one had noticed. The eyes that hadn't been on the bride had been on the beautiful Princess of Surana, but just to be on the safe side straight afterwards she had slipped away below stairs—no guests here, just the caterers who had not made use of the big old-fashioned pantry—to stuff a few more tissues in her bra. Going braless in this dress had not been an option so she had to grin and bear the discomfort it caused her shoulder. Well, it was better than baring her all, which she almost had done!

She stayed in the pantry as long as she could without risking her absence being noticed; the dress dilemma hadn't been the only reason she had taken some time out. A memory of winking dark eyes came into her head and crossly she pushed it away, refusing to give him space in her head—refusing to give him the satisfaction. No man had ever looked at her with such earthy speculation and then to wink as though they shared some sort of secret...or was it that he thought she was a joke? She had maintained an air of cool disdain but inside Eve hadn't felt at all cool!

She had no clue who he was—and she wasn't interested enough to find out, she decided loftily. The guest list was as glittery as was to be expected when the groom was as wealthy and well connected as Charles Latimer, though in true lord-of-the-manor style he had invited all the estate workers and their families, among them a few girls she went to school with. She made no attempt to avoid them but neither did she speak to them.

A minor miracle—helped along by her resisting the temptation of the freely flowing champagne, as alcohol had a way of loosening her tongue—Eve managed to make it through the speeches while maintaining her assigned role of happy daughter of the bride.

By the time the bride and groom took to the floor for their first dance the knot of misery in her chest was a weight so heavy she felt as though it were crushing her, and her face muscles literally ached from the effort of looking pleased and proud while inside she was screaming *no*!

As the applause died away and the other guests began to drift onto the floor she pretended not to see Prince Kamel heading her way—the poor man nudged into doing his duty by Hannah, no doubt—and headed for one of the flower-filled temporary ladies' rooms. The last thing she needed was a sympathy dance!

But what about a sympathy something else…? For some reason the face of one guest popped into her head along with the maverick shameful thought, which she couldn't even blame on alcohol. She gave her bodice a defiant hitch and gritted her teeth, banishing the blatantly sexual features to some dark dusty corner of her mind.

The bathroom was empty—well, she was due a break! Filling a basin with water, she stood there staring at her reflection. What she saw did not improve her mood in the slightest. It had been drizzling when they had transferred from the house to the marquee complex that had been erected on the west lawn for the reception so her hair was no longer sleek. It had frizzed and the strands that had escaped around her hairline had turned into tight corkscrew curls.

She sighed. 'Maybe I should invest in a wig?'

Great, now she was talking to herself. She propped her elbows on the counter top and leaned in close so that her breath fogged the mirror. Standing there with her eyes closed, she patted her hair down as best she could with water, and listened to the soft gurgle as she pulled out the plug and the water drained away.

If she'd had to make a list of the five worst days of her life this one would have been right up there. It was the keeping it in that made everything worse. She'd had to smile through the knowledge that her mother was throwing herself away on a man who was not worthy of her, a man Eve despised, while looking as if she were dressed in a curtain and to top it all *that* man was here watching it happen.

Now what were the chances of that? It was like some horrible cosmic conspiracy! She had turned her head because she had literally felt his eyes on her, which was crazy. But she hadn't been hallucinating; he really was there.

It had been the burst of energising adrenaline resulting from that brief contact and that wink that had got her through the photo shoot, but any benefits had been cancelled out by the fact that every time she had glimpsed him since then he'd been staring at her.

He was rude, he was arrogant and she determinedly ignored him, which was not as easy as it sounded when even across the room and separated by dozens of other people she was painfully conscious of the primitive sexual aura he exuded that had struck her dumb earlier that day. It wasn't just his height or undeniable physical presence that made him stand out among the other men present, it was that rawness, the hint of danger he possessed.

It seemed crazy to Eve that some women were actually attracted by danger, that the whole bad-boy thing turned them on, but not being one of them she went out of her way to avoid him instead.

She opened her eyes and gave her reflection a stern look. 'Come on, Eve, this will all be a memory tomorrow.' Consciously straightening her shoulders, but not so much that it made her bodice slip down—she'd got the hang of it now—she headed for the door.

She had pushed it open a crack when she heard a voice she knew all too well. She peered furtively through the crack, knowing it wasn't one person, it was all three. They always had hunted in a pack and it seemed they still did.

The bullies from her school days no longer wielded the power over her that had made her life a misery but the thought of going out there and facing them right now... No, there were limits to how much 'suck it up and smile' she had left in her—a school reunion with the three witches was just too much to ask of anyone.

Lifting her skirt, she ran for one of the cubicles, closing it just before the three women who like herself had had parents who worked on the estate came in.

'I just love that lippy, Louise.'

There was a clatter as make-up was emptied onto the counter top.

'So Hannah bagged a prince, lucky cow...'

There were murmurs of agreement.

'He's gorgeous, but I think she's put on weight.'

'Oh, definitely.'

'Look who's talking.'

In the cubicle Eve covered her lower face with her hand, not just to protect herself from the cloud of perfume that was drifting her way, but to stifle a gurgle of laughter. She wasn't surprised that her friend inspired jealousy but *fat*…! Hannah was perfect and everyone knew it.

'She's welcome to her prince—it's the hot Italian one I fancy. Now he i*s* fit…with those eyes and that mouth.'

You're obsessed, Eve chided herself. Just because the man is dark, why assume they are talking about him? Italian? Actually, one of the things that had struck her about him had been his Mediterranean colouring… Her green eyes glazed over as she conjured his voice in her head, hearing the slight husk in his deep, sexy drawl, but no accent.

'Is he Italian?'

'Have you never heard of Draco Morelli? Where have you been living?' came the pitying response. 'Honestly, Paula, I sometimes wonder what planet you live on. He's a multibillionaire or something, on all the richest lists.'

'So he's loaded? Better and better. Shame about the scar…but I suppose it isn't that bad.'

'Married?'

Someone giggled. Eve didn't know who by this point as their voices had blended into one high-pitched whine that grated on her nerves. At least one thing was cleared up: there was no longer any question mark over who they were talking about. Once they mentioned the scar she knew that the man the trio were discussing was the one whose stares she had been trying to ignore all day.

'Does it matter?'

The careless response made Eve's lips purse in a silent moue of distaste.

Marriage might not be something she personally aspired to, but if you were going to take vows—and she knew at least two of the women outside her cubicle door were wearing wedding bands—you stayed faithful to those vows.

If not, then what was the point?

She wasn't surprised, given he moved in the same circles as her new stepfather, that this—what had they called him? *Morelli*—had money, but, unlike the trio who were discussing him as though he were a piece of prime juicy steak they contemplated eating, Eve was not impressed.

You could recognise the quality of good tailoring without admiring the person who wore it! Her birth father had money and status and he was a total sleaze. Eve admired talent and intelligence, and there had certainly been intelligence in the dark-eyed stare that had followed her all day, but it had been the sexual challenge in them that had made her stomach muscles quiver.

'A definite plus,' someone admitted. Maybe Emma? Eve speculated. 'But I wouldn't throw him out of bed if he was broke. Imagine him stripped and ready for action...'

During the general laughter and crude comments that followed Eve found herself responding with a mixture of indignation and distaste... It wasn't so much that someone had hijacked her secret fantasy, although that was bad enough, it was that she'd been forced to admit she'd had one, that she had pictured a total stranger naked and sprawled on a bed that bore more than a passing resemblance to her own!

So you wondered what he looked like naked, Eve, big deal, she told herself. Did you think you were the only woman whose creative juices were switched on by his sexual charge?

'He's been staring at me all day, can't take his eyes off me. Have you noticed?' Louise boasted.

Eve's nostrils flared as she hung onto her temper. So he'd been eyeing up all the women—what a sleaze! It was just as well she hadn't felt special…well, not much. She could genuinely say she hadn't *wanted* his attention, but it was one thing not to want it and another to know he pulled the same tired trick with every woman in the room!

'You mean he came on to you? When?'

'I wrote my number on his hand.'

'*No*…how much have you had to drink? What if your Rob had seen?'

'What did he say?'

'He just looked at me and I went shivery! He's got the most incredible eyes… Then he said…'

'*What?* What did he say, Louise?'

The dramatic pause had not just her friends, but Eve in her hiding place, on tenterhooks.

'I could tell by the way he's been looking at me that he wants me. You always can…'

'Yes, but what did he *say*?'

'He said he had an excellent memory and if he wanted to remember a number he would, and then…'

'What? What did he do then?'

'Then he wiped it off!'

Louise had clearly decided this was encouraging. Her cronies, a lot less under her thumb than in the old days, were less sure. The subsequent squabble continued until they found a subject that they all agreed on—they were united in their contempt of the wedding.

'I think in this day and age when people are losing their jobs and everything this sort of lavish display is totally insensitive.'

So why did you come? mouthed Eve from her hiding place. Someone seemed to hear her silent question.

'Yeah, but the champagne is good.'

'She's only the cook.'

'But good-looking. I wouldn't mind looking half as good as E-E-Eve's mum when I'm her age.'

'You've got to hand it to E-E-Eve's mum—she got her man in the end. My mum says they've been at it for years.'

With a militant light in her eyes, Eve reached for the door handle. No one, but *no one*, was about to bad-mouth her mother when she was around and get away with it.

'What about E-E-Evie? What does she think she looks like?'

Eve's hand fell away as she listened to the cruel malicious laughter. It brought the memories flooding back and for a moment she was the misfit stigmatised as a swot and taunted for her stutter.

'And that hair!'

'And the eyebrows, and she's still flat as a pancake, talk about molehills… Do you think she still stutters?'

'I don't know. The snooty cow walked straight past me and acted like I wasn't there. Well, whatever money she is supposed to have made I think that it's exaggerated as she hasn't spent any on make-up. I was right all along—she's definitely a lesbian.'

'You only have to look at her.'

'Definitely.'

'To think we got detention for saying it at school! The girl has no sense of humour.' There was the sound of rustling and another blast of hairspray before someone said, 'That's my mascara.' The sound of the door opening and then, 'She was always full of herself, looking down her nose at us, the little swot.'

Old insults and she'd heard them all before.

The door to the ladies' room closed with a dull clunk and the room fell silent, but Eve stayed inside the cubicle giving them another few minutes just to be on the safe side and let the tears dry.

She lifted a hand to her damp face... How crazy was that? She had sworn that they would not make her cry again, that the bullies who had made her life a misery had long ago lost their power to hurt her.

So why are you hiding in the loo, Eve?

Because she had nothing to prove.

'I'm not hiding.' She was about to slide the latch when a soft reply made her jump.

'I know but it's all right—they've gone.'

The kind voice didn't belong to any of the three faces from the past.

The only person in the otherwise empty ladies' room was a young girl. Even in her flat ballet pumps she was several inches taller than Eve and slender. The encouraging smile she gave when Eve stepped out lit a face that had perfect features.

Eve could feel the girl's warm brown eyes as she walked across to the washbasin. 'Are you all right?'

Eve smiled at the girl's mirror reflection and turned the tap, allowing the warm water to flow over her hands.

'Fine, thanks,' she lied, mortified to hear the wobble in her voice. This was crazy; she was a hard-headed businesswoman, so why was she fighting the sudden and utterly uncharacteristic urge to unburden herself?

The girl continued to look troubled. 'Are you sure?'

What a nice girl. She reminded Eve a little of Hannah at the same age. Not in colouring, as the teenager had raven-black hair, golden-tinged skin and liquid brown eyes, but in the confidence and innate grace that would set her apart from her contemporaries. Eve nodded and the girl walked towards the door.

Her hand was on the handle when she stopped and turned back, her expression earnest. 'My dad,' she began hesitantly. 'Well, he says you shouldn't let them get to you, or at least not let them *see* they get to you. It's the pack instinct—bullies react to the scent of fear, but underneath they're insecure and cowards.'

'Sounds like you have a good dad.'

'I do.' A grin flashed that made her look much younger all of a sudden. 'But he's not perfect.' The grin appeared again. 'Though he thinks he is.'

The girl's grin was contagious.

'Do you mind me asking…? Are you…?'

For the first time that day Eve felt the urge to laugh. She swallowed the tickle of hysteria in her throat, horrified to feel tears pricking her eyelids. 'A lesbian?' Eve finished for her.

'It's fine if you are,' the girl said.

The kid was so sweet, so kind, the contrast with the women's malice so profound that Eve felt the tears press hotly against her eyelids. She blinked hard and stretched a hand to lean heavily on the wall.

The mental exercise she'd employed to lock her emotions in a neat box required energy, and Eve's reserves were severely depleted. If she could have played the scene again she wouldn't have hidden but old habits once learnt were damned hard to break.

'No, I'm not.' The sob when it came emerged from somewhere deep inside her. Eve did not immediately associate it with herself, then another came and another…as all the emotions she had kept under tight control that day suddenly shook loose.

'Stay there. I'll get someone.'

'I'm f-fine...' Eve hiccoughed but the girl had vanished.

CHAPTER FOUR

EVE DIDN'T REALLY expect the girl to return at all but she did, and with the last person in the world she would have expected to see in a ladies' room.

Draco Morelli was the wise father— Oh, my God!

Eve backed away waving a warding hand as she fought to swallow a gulping sob. 'Go away!'

Draco made a swift assessment. 'Keep an eye on the door, Josie, and don't let anyone come in.'

'Okay.' She caught her father's hands and leaned forward to squint at his wrists. 'Did that woman really write her number on your arm? Don't look like that; Year Ten have pictures of you up in their common room. I've grown used to having a *hottie* as a father. Oh, and by the way, she's not a lesbian,' the girl threw over her shoulder as she whisked out of the room.

Draco didn't even blink. 'Always good to know.' He turned back to the weeping woman, who had backed into a corner, her face tear-streaked and her eyes red and puffy.

Marriage had given Draco a deep distrust of female tears. Clare had been able to turn them on and off like a tap and she had perfected the art so that they never smudged her make-up or gave her a blotchy nose. Her weeping was aesthetically perfect.

Comparing Clare's artistic weeping with the sobs that intermittently shook this woman's whole body despite her obvious efforts to control them was like comparing a spring shower with a monsoon. The emotions were genuine, he was conscious of that, along with a twisting of something close to sympathy in his chest, though if he'd been asked to put a name to it he'd have called it indigestion.

Draco had no desire to know the source of this emotional outpouring; he just wanted her to stop crying. In not one of the fantasies he had indulged in to get him through this long and interminably boring day had he pictured her like this.

He had imagined her many other ways, including wearing the striking lingerie, which a few casual enquiries had confirmed she actually designed, and also clad in nothing but an expression of passionate surrender.

His glance drifted over her face, heart-shaped, firm-chinned, her abundant warm-coloured hair springing from a high forehead. He liked his women well groomed and set the bar high, so it was surprising that, even now she was blotchy and tear-sodden, he still found much to please him about her.

He pondered the reason behind his fascination, and decided that the stubborn definition of her soft chin gave her face character and the generous defined line of her arched brows framed eyes that, when not bloodshot, were an almost unique shade of deep green. And of course the mouth that was fuelling his lust-filled fantasies… His wandering gaze stilled on the lush curves and he berated himself mentally after his first thought was about parting those soft pink lips and exploring their moist interior. At his side his long fingers flexed as he pictured himself tenderly brushing aside the curls that clustered around her face.

'I'm fine.' If being totally mortified counted as fine, she thought.

It was some comfort to Draco that she appeared to be gaining a semblance of control.

Maybe you should follow her example, suggested the sardonic voice in his head.

Hard to argue with when he was conscious of the heat pooling in his groin.

She struggled to pull in a deep breath as he continued to stare, making her skin prickle with heat. 'Will you go away?' She injected as much coldness into her voice as was possible while fighting another sob.

More accustomed to having women deliver responses designed to please rather than repel him, Draco took a few seconds to formulate a dignified response.

'I would like nothing better.' It ought to be true, but actually there were several things he would have preferred to do, though none of them was an option while his daughter was outside the door. 'Look, you don't want me here and I don't want to be here—'

'Then go away,' she hurled, wiping her face on her forearm and wishing the floor would open up and swallow her when she caught a glimpse of herself in the mirror behind him. Mortifying enough to make a spectacle of herself but to do it with this man as a witness made it a million times worse.

'My preferred option also,' he bit back, losing his patience. The woman might have a supremely sexy mouth but there were limits to what he was prepared to tolerate to look at it. 'My daughter came to me for help, and Josie retains a childlike belief in my ability to achieve the impossible. I struggle to keep the illusion alive.'

Dry-eyed now, she tilted her chin. 'Odd, she looked like a bright girl.'

She had anticipated an angry response so the appreciative humour that deepened the lines radiating from his spectacular eyes threw her off balance.

'That's better,' he approved. 'So what's the story?'

'What story?' She walked past him to the basin and turned on the water. 'Shouldn't you be going? Someone might come in and, as you see, I'm fine now.'

'Don't worry—Josie will give us some privacy.'

Privacy with this man was the last thing that Eve wanted! The thought sent a fresh flurry of prickles down her spine. 'So what do you expect her to do if someone wants to come in?'

He gave an indifferent shrug. 'She's a very resourceful girl.'

Eve stared at him in the mirror and shook her head. She could hear the pride in his voice; indifference was obviously the last thing he felt when it came to his daughter.

'And you're a really weird sort of father, not that I know anything about fathers.' Wishing the admission unsaid, she bent her head and splashed water on her blotchy face.

When she lifted her head again he was standing right there beside her, close enough for her to be conscious of the warmth of his hard, lean body, with one of the neatly folded individual hand towels that were stacked beside the linen basket in his hand.

She stared at it as though she'd never seen a towel before while the water from her hands dripped on the floor. She wasn't conscious of lifting her gaze, but as her eyes drifted slowly over the hard angles of his face she was suddenly aware of the increased volume of a low static hum in her ears.

This close she could appreciate just how evenly textured his golden-toned skin was, shadowed now by a light dusting of dark stubble that almost hid the scar next to his mouth.

She felt a sudden and almost uncontrollable urge to lift her hand and touch the place where she knew it was and trace the line…

'So, you don't have a dad, then?'

Like a sleepwalker coming to, she started, her raised hand moving jerkily and snatching the towel from him without a word. Under cover of a glare, she fought a debilitating wave of trembling weakness.

'What, is this research for your next book?' she snapped.

'Well, they do say everyone has one in them, but actually you just interest me.'

His comment whipped away her protective camouflage. Feeling horribly exposed and yet, more worryingly, excited, she dabbed her face with the towel. 'I'm not at all interesting, Mr Morelli.'

His sable brows lifted. 'You know my name.'

'It came up in the conversation.'

'Ah, yes, the conversation,' he mused slowly. 'So

those charming friends of yours, what did they say that upset you so much?'

'Not friends,' she flashed, then, seeing his expression, she lowered her eyes and added more moderately, 'We went to school together, the little village school, and then—'

'Here, you missed a bit...' He took a corner of the towel she still held and, leaning in to her, dabbed a spot beside her mouth. Then he dabbed it again...and again...

Eve, who had been standing like a small statue, her eyes trained straight ahead, while admiring his very nice ears, heard a whimper escape her lips and hastily turned it into a cough.

'Secondary school,' she finished faintly.

'That cough sounds bad.' Draco was happy to go along with the pretence for now, but was curious why it apparently bothered her so much that there was such a dramatic level of sexual chemistry between them. Unless... A furrow indented his brow as he realised that just because she had no partner here did not necessarily mean there wasn't one somewhere in the background.

The possibility she was unavailable dragged the

corners of his mouth downwards in a brooding, dissatisfied curve.

Her eyes slid away from his. 'A tickle in my throat.' It sounded less inflammatory than 'a starburst in my belly'.

'Relax,' he ordered.

Eve bit back a laugh.

'You might as well tell me what they said, you know, because otherwise Josie will, and if my daughter has been traumatised I'd like to know up front.'

'Traumatised!' She was shocked by the suggestion and then it dawned on her that his interest arose from parental anxiety and not, as she had thought... Well, what did you think, Evie—that he found you fascinating? That he wanted to know what made you tick or just that he wanted 'to get in your pants?

In your dreams. She sighed and then thought wryly that was probably the only way he'd ever appear in her bed! It was ridiculous to try and pretend that this man hadn't awoken some dormant responses in her or that he wasn't the domineering, controlling type that she was never going to get involved with. He might make an appearance

in her fantasies but in real life—no way! He might
make a lousy lover but at least he seemed to be a
good and concerned father.

'Your daugh… Josie wasn't involved… I wasn't
involved in what just happened in here.' Eve was
horrified that he seemed to suspect that his daughter had witnessed some sort of slanging match.
Or maybe even a brawl. 'Really,' she assured him
earnestly. 'They didn't even know I was here and I
didn't know your daughter was here either. It was
just a case of eavesdroppers hearing bad things
about themselves… We didn't get on at school
either.'

'They look a lot older than you…'

He caught her look and added, 'Josie pointed
them out when she was dragging me in here. Why
would their jealousy of you make you cry?'

God, why didn't Josie come and drag him out
again—right now? Eve glanced at the doorway,
willing the girl to appear, but it remained empty.
She sighed again. The quickest way to get him
out of here seemed to be to satisfy his curiosity
and go three seconds without breaking down like
some sort of neurotic basket case.

'That had nothing to do with them. It was just

a combination of champagne, jet lag and...' She stopped, an arrested expression appearing on her face as she belatedly processed his comment. 'They aren't *jealous*.' Spiteful and insensitive, granted... 'Why would you think they were jealous of me?'

He looked amused by the question. 'Let me see. You are a success and you are beautiful and they are...' His lips twisted into a grimace of contempt as he recalled the blonde with the unlikely orange tan who had thrust her chest in his face and written her number on his hand, embarrassing all those who had witnessed the action.

Draco had not been embarrassed but he had been offended and annoyed.

'Not.'

He thought she was beautiful?

'And you did not drink any champagne.'

Her accusing green stare settled on his face; it was nice just for once to be the one on the offensive. 'How do you know?'

'I'm an observant man.'

Her eyes narrowed. 'You were watching me!' she flung, quivering with a combination of outrage and excitement that tied her stomach in knots and brought a flush to her pale skin.

'And you knew I was.' His retort was unanswerable for someone who was not a good liar. 'It is the game men and women play, *cara*,' he drawled.

Eve felt as if she had just stepped out of the training pool into the deep end. She struggled to fight her way through the panic that was closing in on her and remain calm and in control. 'I'm not playing games.'

He looked at her for a long moment, acknowledging a flicker of uncertainty as the extraordinary possibility that she was telling the truth occurred to him. She could not be *that* inexperienced, surely? But looking deep into those big emerald eyes, he saw she wasn't trying to hide anything—or perhaps she didn't know how...?

A word popped into his head: *innocence.*

He straightened up, pulling away from her in more than the physical sense. He had thought they were on the same page but he had been wrong; he had seen that sultry mouth but not the emotional baggage that came with it. It was a good thing he had discovered his error now, before things had gone too far, he told himself.

She was high maintenance, and he was a bastard who had no intention of changing. Always better in his experience to call a spade a spade.

'Will you do something for me?' he asked.

He was not about to make an indecent proposal with his daughter just outside the door but even so her heartbeat kicked into a higher gear. 'That depends.'

'Smile and try not to look so tragic.'

She stiffened, her spine snapping to attention. 'Pardon me?'

'I'd like to stay a hero for as long as I can in my daughter's eyes, so I'd be grateful if you could suck it up and look like I waved my magic wand and made everything better. It's not as if you're the only one who doesn't like weddings. I suspect with me it's that they remind me too much of my own,' he admitted with a frankness she was beginning to find disturbing.

It was a day he was able to think about with a degree of objectivity now, but for a long time it hadn't been that way. Now he was able to admit that he had known halfway through exchanging his vows that he was making the biggest mistake of his life, and it was doubtful it would even have got that far if his parents hadn't been so against it, and delivered an ultimatum.

He had been twenty and had thought he knew everything. Their parental disapproval had been like a red rag to a bull, and what better way to display his maturity than to get married against their wishes and show them how wrong they were?

'Suck it up?' she repeated in a low, dangerous voice. 'Suck it up? What the hell do you think I've been doing all d-d-day? As for your marriage, I...I...spare me the details.' She glared at him, daring him to comment on her stutter. These days it rarely surfaced but she was always conscious that it could at any moment—and it was his fault that it just had.

Eve felt something snap inside her. 'You think you don't like weddings, let me tell you,' she huffed, 'about my day!' She reached inside the bodice of her dress and after a grunt produced a wad of tissues, which she waved at him. 'Did you have to stuff your bra full of tissues to keep your dress up? Did you have to watch your mother, who is the best, *totally* best person you know, marry a man who is so far beneath her in every way?' Eve's voice dropped a husky octave but shook with the strength of the emotion that gripped her as she concluded, 'And it wouldn't even be happening now if the scumbag hadn't got her pregnant!'

For about three seconds she felt the intense relief of getting it off her chest…and then she looked at the tissues in her hand and gulped quite literally. The wave of horror that followed made her want to vanish… What had she been thinking of, telling a total stranger such private things?

Her green eyes lifted to his face, her insides churning sickly. 'If you tell anyone I'll—'

'Be forced to have me killed. Don't worry— your secret is safe with me,' Eve heard him drawl with teeth-clenching sarcasm.

'The idea is growing on me,' she declared grimly.

Forgetting the cold shoulder he had intended to present to her, he grinned. 'I'm curious—have you got any more tissues down there or is what remains all you?'

She pressed her hand to the neckline of her strapless gown; without the extra padding to fill it he had a view all the way down to her waist and he was certainly looking.

'You're hateful!' Eve looked at the wad of tissues and threw them at him.

Laughing, he reached out and caught them. 'Seriously.' Actually he had been *seriously* impressed by the view of her small but perfect breasts like plump little apples in their lacy covering. He could just imagine them filling his hand—only they wouldn't because she was high maintenance. She was an innocent… Mmm, *how innocent, exactly…?*

He didn't want to know. All right, maybe he did—virgins of her age were a bit like unicorns: the things of fables.

'So what have you got against Charlie Latimer?' The guy was successful, solvent and as far as he knew had no major vices like drink, drugs or gambling, yet her animosity had been toxic in its intensity.

'So you don't know he's been having an affair with my mum for years? That makes you something of a rarity.' Could you sound any more bitter, Eve?

'I don't listen to gossip, but I do know that relationships are complex and it's hard to judge what makes one work from the outside.'

'They didn't have a *relationship.* She was his bit on the side. She doesn't *have* to marry anyone, let alone him! I'd have looked after her. I *wanted* to look after her.'

'You're very possessive.'

'Protective,' she flashed back, angry at the inference and his sardonic expression.

'Don't you think that maybe your mother has earned the right to make her own decisions and her own mistakes...?'

She cast a simmering glance up at his lean face. 'What business is it of yours anyway?'

'None at all. I thought you wanted my input.'

'Well, I don't!'

'I stand corrected.'

She pulled herself up to her full height and, bristling with dignity, looked pointedly at the route to the door he was blocking. 'If you don't mind...? And don't worry.' She flashed him a wide insincere smile, her eyes shooting daggers. 'I will smile, but I'd prefer not to be seen coming out of the ladies' room with you.'

'It might make the world look at you in a different light.'

She narrowed her eyes and said with fierce distaste, 'You mean people will see me as a tart.'

'No, I mean they might think you actually have a life.'

She sucked in a breath of outrage. 'I have a perfectly good life already and I don't give a damn what people think.'

'If that were true you wouldn't give a damn what people think if we walk out that door together.'

Teeth clenched in sheer frustration, she glared up at him. He couldn't have looked smugger if... if... No, he simply couldn't have looked smugger. 'Just wait here.'

'Shall I count to a hundred?'

Responding to this with a disdainful sniff, she tossed her head and pushed through the doorway, pausing only to fling a 'Thank you!' over her shoulder.

He didn't count to a hundred. Instead he thought about what had just happened. Running the scene through his head, little snippets of the conversation making him frown, others smile. It had clearly hurt her to say thank you, and Draco felt a faint twinge of guilt as he knew he didn't deserve it. The only cry of help he'd responded to was his daughter's. He'd only come in here for Josie, because he wanted her to think he was a good guy, but in truth he wasn't. If he had seen an hysterical woman crying in the bathroom, his instinct would not have been to wade in and help, it would have been to walk in the opposite direction very fast.

He had his life streamlined so that he could focus on what was important—he did not get involved.

The women standing outside reading the 'out of order' sign that was pinned to the door looked at him wide-eyed when he emerged.

Ignoring their astonished stares, he unpinned the sign written in the pink lipstick his daughter was wearing and nodded.

'Everything is back to normal.'

Which was a good thing. Eve Curtis had even more issues than he had imagined; the man who got her would need a medal and a degree in counselling.

CHAPTER FIVE

DRACO JOINED HIS daughter, who was sitting at an empty table beside the dance floor. 'The notice on the door was a nice touch.'

'Is everything all right, Dad?'

'Fine.' He reached out a hand to ruffle her hair but Josie got to her feet

'She's available; I checked.'

Draco looked down, not so very far now. Over the past ten months his daughter had grown ten inches and had gone from being a sweet, slightly chubby five-feet-one twelve-year-old to a slender, leggy thirteen-year-old; still sweet but to his parental eye worryingly mature, with the sort of coltish good looks that had already drawn two offers of modelling contracts.

Draco was just relieved he hadn't had to come the heavy parent over the latter; Josie had plans for her future that did not include becoming the face of anything.

'Who is available?' He glanced down and noticed for the first time that his daughter was holding a cocktail. He winced and blamed Eve for taking his eye off the ball. Just what was the woman's problem? He slung a quick glance across the room and sure enough she was still acting as if she were at a wake, not a wedding reception. God, no wonder she had been bullied; she was one of those people who simply couldn't blend into the background, and didn't try either. She stood out in a room of a hundred—or in this case nearer five.

He reached for the drink. 'I don't think so, angel.'

'You know something, Dad, you have serious trust issues. It's only a mocktail.' She turned the stick in the glass of brightly coloured but non-alcoholic contents and offered with a grin, 'Try if you don't believe me.'

His expressive lips twisted into a moue of distaste. 'I'll pass.'

'So about Eve, Dad.'

He shook his head wryly. *About Eve*—it was more a case of a detour around Eve. She was an emotional storm. He caught his daughter's look and said defensively, 'What about Eve?'

'I said she's available.'

His daughter was teasing, but under her smiles was she really…? He wasn't entirely sure, but one thing he was sure of was that this was a conversation he did not want to have.

'Is that boy a friend of yours?' He angled a narrow look towards the young man who was making his tipsy way across the dance floor towards his daughter. Recognising the warning, the kid abruptly changed direction.

'Good try, Dad.'

'Try at what?'

'At changing the subject.'

'What subject would that be?'

Josie rolled her eyes before directing a finger across the room to where Eve was standing. 'She's all alone and you should go and talk to her. Or are you scared?' his daughter, who thought she knew what buttons to press, speculated innocently. The hell of it was that five times out of ten she did and he could see those odds narrowing as she got older.

'I know a lot of men are scared of rejection,' she added.

Draco, who didn't have much experience of

rejection, looked amused; women's magazines had a lot to answer for. 'So how do you know that men are scared of rejection?'

'Clare told me.'

His half-smile faded. 'Since when do you call your mother Clare?' he asked sternly.

'She asked me to—she says now that I'm taller than her being called Mum makes her feel old.' Seeing his expression, Josie touched her father's arm. 'She can't help it, you know. Some people are just—'

'Self-centred and selfish.' Draco frowned, regretting the bitter words the moment they were uttered. After the divorce he had been determined not to bad-mouth his ex-wife to their daughter and always felt guilty as hell when he failed. He did not want to be the sort of parent who used their kid as a bargaining chip and asked them to take sides.

'Relax, Dad, you're not telling me anything that I didn't work out for myself years ago. So are you scared…? You've been staring at her all day—yes, Dad, you have. She is *the* Eve in Eve's Temptation. Brains and beauty. Oh, before you say it—'

'What was I about to say?'

'Beauty isn't all about long legs and boobs, Father.'

Always good to know that your daughter thought you were shallow and sexist. 'I am aware of that.'

'And you obviously fancy her so don't let me cramp your style. Go for it, Dad.'

'Thank you very much.'

His daughter ignored the irony. 'I think you need a challenge.'

'Being your father makes every day a challenge.'

'I'm a far better daughter than you deserve.' She grinned and for a moment looked more like his little girl again. Draco pushed away the wave of nostalgia and reminded himself that nothing stayed the same.

'I'm not going to contest that one.' He touched her cheek. 'How about you let me worry about my social life, kiddo?'

Her childish brow furrowed. 'I just don't want to see you lonely. I'm not going to be at home for ever, you know, and you're not getting any younger.'

Feeling every day of his thirty-three years, Draco allowed his daughter to pull him onto the dance floor. Eve had already gone.

* * *

Having delivered the car and the keys to Draco, his driver squeezed his bulk into the passenger seat of the Mini beside his wife. Draco stepped smartly to one side as the Mini reversed, sending up a cloud of gravel, and shot off down the drive with a honk of the horn.

A smile played across the firm line of his lips as he watched the car vanish, narrowly avoiding a collision with one of the catering vans that were beginning to leave. On balance Draco was glad the husband and not the wife was his driver.

He strolled back towards the Elizabethan manor, which was impressively backlit now the light had faded by some state-of-the-art laser technology. Less high tech but equally attractive were the trees surrounding the house, which had been artistically sprinkled with white fairy lights for the occasion. There was no sign of Josie, who had said she'd be only five minutes when she had gone back to make up a doggie bag for her cousin, fifteen minutes ago.

Overhead a helicopter took off, and he sighed. It would have been easier to make the return journey by the same means of transport in which he had arrived, but the last time he had landed in the meadow at the timbered farmhouse where his ex-model sister lived the bucolic life of a hobby farmer with her banker husband, she had complained that her hens had stopped laying.

It did not seem very scientific, but then neither was naming a load of hens who all looked identical to him and assigning them individual personalities, so rather than risk getting in her bad books again, as she helped out a lot with Josie, having her to stay when he was out of town, he had decided to drop Josie off by car before driving back to London himself.

Philosophical about being kept waiting by his daughter, he had positioned himself beneath the illuminated canopy of a tall oak to wait for Josie just as a minibus filled with guests from the village set off, leaving behind three figures on the gravel.

'Who is he calling drunk?' the one who had written her number on his arm slurred, waving her fists at the bus.

Another sat down on the floor and took off her shoes. 'My feet hurt. Louise, why did you have to swear at him?'

Moving back into the shadow, an expression of distaste twisting his lean, patrician features, Draco placed a supportive hand on his neck and rotated his head in an effort to relieve some of the stiffness afflicting his muscles.

The first exercise having failed, he was rolling his shoulders when a figure appeared in the illuminated doorway—not Josie, but one he recognised. It wasn't hard as she was still wearing the full-length bridesmaid dress, but now it was topped by a lacy shrug that had little cap sleeves that covered her bare shoulders and was buttoned up to her throat, concealing everything else.

He watched as she glanced to right and left as though looking for someone and then began to walk towards him, only not him, she couldn't see him, yet a man could be excused for thinking it was a sign.

A man could also be accused of spinning the situation because of the ache in his groin. He sighed and stepped deeper into the shadows. His trouble was he had gone too long without; there had only been the one night since ending things with Rachel.

There could have been more but he had not

made the effort—not that there was much effort involved. He had the number on his phone of a young politician who was attractive, ambitious and discreet. She had a busy schedule, was opposed to cumbersome emotional baggage, and her Brussels base was an advantage, not a problem.

'Here she comes. E-E-E-Evie.' If the sniggered whisper was loud enough for him, the odds were that Evie had heard it too.

Draco slid the phone back into his pocket as he felt a sudden rush of anger. If he had paused to think, he would have been surprised by the white-hot intensity of it, but he didn't pause. Instead he stepped out of the shadows where two strides brought him to Eve's side. Without a word he grabbed her by the arm and jerked her towards him.

Soft and warm, she collided with him, her gentle curves fitting perfectly into the angles of his body.

She was too shocked to even cry out; her eyes flew wide, her pupils dilating dramatically as she looked up into the face of the man who held her. She let out a tiny fluttery sigh, stiffening as almost casually he slid his free hand around her waist, his fingers spreading across her ribcage

from her waist to just beneath her breast, possessively, as if he had the right.

'What are you doing?' The question proved her
brain was working... The rest of her body she
wrote off, as it was clearly reacting independently.
The heat that made her skin burn was seeping into
her blood, so that she felt light-headed, and the
sensual fog in her brain made it hard to think—
so she just stopped trying.

Why bother when it was a fight she was going
to lose? Because she really wanted to taste him,
and it was all she could think about.

He bent in closer, brushing her cheek with his
lips, holding her eyes all the time. His stare was
hypnotic; she couldn't have broken eye contact
even if she'd wanted to and there was a big...no,
a massive question mark over that.

'I'm going to kiss you—are you all right with
that?'

No...one word, how hard was that? That's all
you have to say, she told herself firmly.

'Someone will see,' she whispered instead.

'They're meant to, so shut up, *cara*, and don't
have another panic attack.'

The comment roused Eve to lethargic indignation. 'I don't have panic attacks. Let me go!' It was weak and way overdue, but at least she'd made a protest—she could tell herself later *I tried to stop him.*

Man up, Eve, take responsibility—you want this.

'What the hell do you think you're doing, Draco?' Saying his name had been a mistake as suddenly everything seemed intimate, more personal.

'Relax and don't hit me; we have an audience. I am once and for all going to lay to rest any doubts about your sexuality.' He touched the side of her jaw. 'Don't look.'

She lifted her gaze to his, and the dark passion-glazed look in her eyes sent a surge of power through his veins.

'Look where?' She could no longer pretend she wanted to look at anything but him.

Her voice had dropped a sexy octave, the sound possessing a tactile quality that made him hungry to feel her small hands on his skin...exploring...

'Do you have doubts about my s-sexuality?'

'Not a one,' he said against her lips. 'I hate the idea of you stuttering for anyone else.'

Her stutter was the bane of her existence and

he was acting as though it were a gift! 'You don't have to do this.' But of course if he didn't she might die, although to the women watching them she knew it already looked as though they were kissing. 'I really don't care what they think.' But it might be nice to wipe the smiles off their smug faces.

'Actually I *do* have to do this,' he muttered raggedly.

They were both breathing so fast she could not separate the sounds or even the heartbeats. She gave a little nod, her breathless moan of anticipation barely audible.

'I have wanted to kiss you since this morning when you threw your bra at me.'

His eyelashes cast shadows along the crest of his cheekbones and through her half-closed eyes they looked like solid blocks of colour. 'That feels like years ago...' The words were soft sibilant sighs, hardly audible above her tortured shallow breaths. 'Well...?'

'Well what?'

'Are you going to find out...how it feels to—?'

The rest of her words were lost in the warmth of his mouth. He explored her mouth, his tongue probing and his lips moving against hers with sensuous expertise. The pressure of the kiss bent her backwards against his supporting arm and she straightened up again as his head lifted like a sapling when the wind died.

He was still close and breathing hard; they both were. Through the mesh of her lashes she could see the fine texture of his olive-toned skin, the darkened stubble thicker now on the surface of his jaw and lower face, the gold tips on the end of his thick jet-black eyelashes. A shiver of sensation rippled through her body, then another and another...

'So was that your good deed for the day?' she murmured.

Draco, who had really fought his baser instincts to keep the kiss under control, just nodded. It had been a mistake to kiss her; all it had done was make him realise what he was missing and that he wanted her more than ever.

'Yeah, and now that our first kiss is out of the way...' He leaned in again, the gleam in his dark eyes warning her of his intent.

This time the kiss was very different. With considerably less finesse, less control, the wildness scared Eve on one level and on another excited her unbearably. She wanted everything he was doing and more. The knowledge shocked even as it made her arch into him.

She could feel his arousal rock hard against her belly as he moulded her against him, sealing their bodies at hip level. Then while he continued to plunder her mouth with a raw hunger of bruising intensity Draco's big hands moved over her body.

She could feel the heat of his hand through the silk of her dress as it moved up and down her thigh. While his other kneaded and moulded the aching peak of one small breast.

It didn't even cross her mind that they were standing in full view of anyone who happened by. She couldn't think beyond the throbbing ache of need between her thighs and when it became too much to bear and as what was left of her control broke she grabbed the back of his neck with both hands and pulled his face in closer.

Eve kissed him back with an urgency, a wildness, that matched his. She clung to him like a limpet as he staggered back, struggling to keep his balance while she pulled at his clothes with greedy hands, trailing kisses across his face, down the strong column of his neck then moving back to his mouth.

When she slid her hands under his shirt he gasped, then moaned. Eve felt his ribcage lift as he sucked in a breath then held it as he grabbed both of her hands, which were sliding down the corrugated muscles of his belly, and dragged them away.

He stood back, looking down at her for a moment, at the wanton picture she made. It had been the feeling of her eager hands sliding over his damp, satiny smooth skin that had almost made his control snap, and it was only the knowledge that his daughter could be one of those interesting passers-by to witness this that made him hold back.

'Well, I think that might have done the trick,' he gasped, still fighting for control.

Oh, God, oh, God, oh, God!

The cry was in the vault of her skull. Her lips thankfully stayed closed and trembling as Eve watched him drag his shirt together, tucking it into his trousers.

'Are you all right?' He felt a slug of unwelcome guilt, she looked so damned fragile standing there.

She took several shaky steps backwards, only stopping when her back made contact with a tree. Lifting her chin, she directed what she hoped was a look of cold disdain, but was more than likely breathless shock and confusion, at his lean face.

He wasn't touching her but there was a fierce intensity in his rigid attitude that made her stomach muscles vibrate.

'I'm not going to have sex with you to prove I'm not a lesbian.'

'Oh, I think you proved that already seeing as your friends have left. And it is always polite, *cara*, to wait to be asked first.'

She had no defence against the mortified rush of colour that bathed her body in a guilty glow. 'Pity you didn't ask first before you mauled me about like that. And you can quit with all that Italian *cara* stuff; it's incredibly cheesy.'

'To be accurate I think we should call it mutual…mauling,' he mused, the smouldering glow in his deep-set eyes sparking as he added, 'And to be honest that didn't go quite the way I anticipated. Sorry—' he glanced over his shoulder '—but Josie could be here any minute.'

Just when she thought she could not feel any

more humiliated, she tossed her head. 'It was only a kiss.'

His brows lifted and he barked a dry laugh. 'If you think that was *only a kiss, cara*, I can't wait to see your version of *just sex*!'

'There won't be any just sex! No sex at all!' Turning on her heel, she could hear his soft laughter following her.

CHAPTER SIX

IF HER MUM had been around this wouldn't be happening because Eve knew that Sarah would have taken one look at her daughter's face and said, 'No way are you driving, my girl—you're in no fit state.'

It wouldn't have mattered what Eve said because that was what mothers did: they stopped their daughters driving even if they were perfectly capable—or she would have done if she'd been there and not off on her honeymoon with her new husband.

Eve gave a self-pitying sniff as she trudged on, finding it easy to lay her present predicament at the door of Charlie Latimer. She decided to give it until that next bend, because how frustrating would it be if she turned back only to later realise that she had actually been within a few hundred yards of the main road and hopefully some help or at least some place with a phone signal?

She was trying her phone again when she heard the car in the distance and felt a stab of relief. But by the time the distant light had become dazzling the relief had morphed into apprehension; if this were a crime drama she'd be the body in the first scene, the one that normally made her want to shout at the screen, How could you be so stupid?

She took a deep breath. This was real life, most people were not homicidal maniacs and she was not about to get into a car with a stranger. She just wanted to ask if they could contact a local garage to come and pick her and her car up...yes, that was definitely the sensible option.

The big low car slowed and, heart beating hard, Eve carried on walking, though more slowly, projecting as much confidence as possible as you should when you were alone in the dark in the middle of nowhere... For goodness' sake, Eve, Surrey is hardly the last wilderness! she scorned.

'Are you totally insane?'

It was not the conversational comment that made her spin around directing her wide-eyed stare at the driver of the car, but the deep voice with that tactile 'once heard never ever forgotten' quality. Her stomach reacted by going into a deep dive while simultaneously every square inch of her skin prickled with an appalling awareness that was painful in its intensity.

Her head was immediately filled with thoughts of his mouth crashing down on hers, his warm lips teasing, tormenting… With a massive effort she reined in her imagination and her indiscriminate hormones, managing to focus on the here and now.

The painful truth here was that in some ways a homicidal maniac might have been easier to cope with.

The engine was still running as she took a deep breath, lifting a hand to her face against the glare of the headlights as the driver's door was flung open and the occupant vaulted out.

It was impossible to read his expression, but his body language was less of a struggle. His tall, lean frame was rigid, projecting none of the languid, mocking attitude that got under her skin, but something that approached anger.

She squared her shoulders. Some people might conclude it was a sort of cosmic conspiracy or fate that kept on throwing her into this man's path. Eve, who believed a person was in charge of their own fate, thought it was more of a bad day getting worse!

A lot worse.

'What are you doing here?' Not your loud voice, Eve, warned the critic in her head. As he took a step closer and she fought the urge to mirror his action with several back she got sucked in once again by the entire in-your-face physical thing he had going on. If his voice was hard to forget the rest of him was...she released a tight fractured sigh and thought...stupendous.

'I was passing...?'

She did not respond to the dry wit but then as a shaft of moonlight fell directly across his face she saw he wasn't smiling either; each fascinating hollow and carved sybaritic angle of his incredible face was set in a grim line of cold accusation that set her chin up another defensive notch.

'Are you stalking m-me?' It was not hard to visualise him as a sleek predator but she, Eve reminded herself, was not anyone's prey. Despite her intention to cloak her comment with a believable level of amused indifference, she finished on a stutter.

Cut yourself some slack, Eve. There probably

wasn't a woman on the entire planet who could laugh at the idea of being pursued by this man... and they hadn't been kissed by him—or kissed him back.

She closed the door on that memory, but not before her insides had dissolved and her core temperature had risen several painful degrees.

'If I was stalking you, you're making it damned easy.'

'You're calling me easy?' Why not just leave your foot in your mouth, Eve? It will save you time and energy, she thought with an internal groan.

'Easy?'

The echo carried a note she tried to place as his dark eyes went from her face to the near-empty minor road. She turned her head, wondering if he had seen another car.

Five miles, Draco estimated, if not more since he had seen another vehicle, and that off-roader had turned down a farm track. He wouldn't be on it himself if he hadn't been dropping off Josie at her English cousin's house, and what would Eve have done then...?

Eve tensed as his attention refocused on her face.

'No, you're bloody hard work. Just get in the damned car.'

'That won't be necessary, thank you. I don't want to be a nuisance, but if you could inform a garage that I broke down. This is a short cut.' Hearing the defensiveness in her own voice, Eve frowned. For the past half-hour she had been contemplating turning back as each successive bend in the road did not reveal the main road—but there was no need to tell him that.

His brows lifted as he slid a phone from his pocket, wishing leaving her standing here in the middle of nowhere was an option.

Liar, said the voice in his head. He hadn't got excited by the idea of making out in a car since his teens, but for some reason this woman, with her prickles and her lush lips and her hungry eyes, had made him ache in a way that made self-delusion useful. After all, what was the point over-analysing something that was as simple as sex? Especially as with her he knew it would be stupendous!

'Ever heard of mobile phones?' Ever heard of avoiding someone with emotional high maintenance written all over her face? He detoured around his own internal question and waved his phone at her—trying to ignore the way the softening effect of the dark copper-toned curls that framed her face made her appear younger and more vulnerable.

'Ever heard of black spots where you get no signal?' she returned seamlessly. Did the man think she was a total idiot?

No, he just thinks you're easy, Eve—with good reason! The door opened on the memory still raw, still recent, still mortifying and, yes, still wildly exciting, submerging her in a tidal wave of hot, lustful longing against which her only defence was to shove her trembling hands into her pockets and look away.

She could not remember feeling this out of control for…well, ever. She didn't like it, and she didn't like him. No, not liking him was too mild an emotion; she hated him.

Draco's ebony brows twitched into a line above his masterful nose as he slid the phone back into his pocket without looking at it. He was trying not to see the visible tremors that shook her slender frame under the double-breasted jacket that looked at least two sizes too big for her.

'Get in!' he snapped, fighting off an irrational surge of tenderness; combined with the lust that still circulated hotly through his veins, it made for a contradictory and uncomfortable mix. It was a massive mistake to equate small and delicate with vulnerable or in need of protection—she was as tough as nails.

Or she'd like the world to think she was.

Ignoring the mental addition, he added with silky sarcasm, 'Unless you would prefer to walk? Or possibly wait for a serial killer? They do say that they come along in twos, or is that buses?'

Her scornful glance swept upwards from his polished toes but she only made it as far as his waist and stalled. At some point, like her, Draco had changed. The dark jeans he now wore fitted just as perfectly as the tailored trousers of his morning suit, though the cut of the denim emphasised his lean hips and the muscularity of his thighs.

Swallowing past the sudden aching occlusion in her throat, she wrenched her eyes clear, gave a scornful snort and angrily retorted, 'You've never caught a bus in your life!' She stopped, frowning darkly as her accusation drew a startled laugh from him. 'And statistically speaking—'

The pistol-shot snap of Draco's long fingers made Eve jump and indicated his opinion of statistics and his diminishing patience levels. She was glad of the interruption as it was hard to focus on statistics when she was thinking how it felt to be plastered up close against those iron-hard thighs, feeling the shocking imprint of a rock-hard arousal on her belly.

He gave a sigh, intoning wearily, 'Get in, Eve. I've better things to do than stand here arguing the toss.'

Eve, who had been swaying slightly, blinked hard. She knew about red mists but the one that floated in her brain clouding good sense was darker and it had warmth and depth and— No, don't wrap it up, Eve, she told herself impatiently. It's just lust; get over yourself. So the man knows how to kiss?

'Thank you, but I've said if you could—'

He raised an ironic brow and she stopped, catching her full upper lip between her white teeth as she gave a sigh and surrendered, if not to the dark mist, then to the practicalities of her situation. So she accepted a lift from him—what was the worst that could happen?

She brushed a strand of curling chestnut hair from her eyes. The only thing she'd achieved when she'd looked in the engine earlier had been a bang on the head, which had shaken half her hair loose. Of course it had gone into frizz mode immediately. Her eyes went to his dark head. After they'd kissed his hair had been sexily ruffled. Now it was smooth and sleek and yet it was still sexy.

'That's very kind of you—' Her eyes connected with his and she stopped speaking, her heart beating hard and fast. There was nothing that could be even loosely termed as kind in his eyes right now; the feral glow made her insides dissolve.

She sounded like a prim schoolmistress and she looked— His eyes slid of their own volition to the full curve of her cushiony lips, and he groaned silently. He recalled how she kissed like a sex-starved angel, and gritted his teeth against the ache in his groin that packed the kick of a mule.

'I'm not kind.'

Eve gave her head a tiny shake, causing a curling tendril to attach itself to her mouth, and she detached the strands with an impatient frown.

In his seat before her Draco leant across, pulling away the jacket draped over the back of the passenger seat before she leaned back. His hand touched her shoulder as he slung it into the back, even that light contact sending an electrical surge through her body.

She survived the brush of his eyes, breathing through the moment and even managing to acknowledge his action with a slight nod despite the swirling confusion in her brain.

As he hit the ignition the space was filled with a classic jazz ballad. Eve exhaled, covering her mouth with her hand to disguise her sigh of relief—she wouldn't have to make conversation.

Then he turned it off.

They had driven a few minutes when he broke the silence.

'Will you fasten your jacket?'

She didn't fight the childish urge to challenge everything he said or question it too deeply. 'Why? I'm warm.'

The comment drew a rumble of laughter from

his throat, but, bemused and desperately hiding her reaction to the nerve-shredding effect of being in close physical proximity to him, Eve turned her head and slung him a scowl.

'I'm missing the irony.'

'You make your living selling underwear but you don't wear your own products.'

She was tired and stressed and it took a few moments for his meaning to penetrate. When it did she grabbed the corners of her jacket and pulled them together.

'You mean I'm not an underwear model. Well, for the record, most women aren't and I make underwear for normal women.'

'Make but not wear.'

'I...I had a very minor surgery and the bra strap chafes.' The Australian doctor had been reassuring about the mole he'd said looked innocent, but to be safe he'd whipped it off and sent it for analysis.

'Minor?'

'A mole removal, but it was nothing sinister.'

His brow smoothed as he slid a sideways look at her face. 'With your skin you should plaster on factor fifty.'

'I'm not an idiot.'

'That's open to debate.' What wasn't was her delicious, soft, smooth pale skin; it would be nothing short of criminal to expose it to the harshening effects of the sun. 'Statistically speaking, someone with your colouring—'

'I am not ginger; it's chestnut.'

Colour aside, it was an essential part of his fantasies.

'Well, statistically—'

'Do you know how boring people who quote statistics are?'

He adopted an expression of unconvincing confusion as he consulted the rear-view mirror. 'I never quote statistics,' he explained. 'I make them up—no one ever knows the difference and you sound informed and intelligent.'

'Seriously?'

'Totally,' he confirmed. 'You should try it. You'd be amazed at how few people question a statistic.'

Eve bit her quivering lip, then, losing her fight, broke into peals of laughter.

She had a great laugh, when she wasn't feeling bitter and twisted and sexually frustrated. He couldn't believe now that he had actually almost convinced himself she was a virgin. He realised that Eve Curtis could be fun outside bed, not that his interest in her extended beyond the bedroom, he told himself.

Wiping her eyes, she turned to him. 'So the next time I find myself losing an argument I should make up a statistic.'

'You have to keep an element of realism and you have to believe what you say.'

'You mean,' she cut back slickly, 'you have to be a good liar.'

'That goes without saying...'

'Like you.'

'I could say I'm always honest but I might be lying.' Eve recognised the crossroads they were approaching; it was the one where she always nursed a secret fear of taking the wrong turning and ending up in Wales.

She told him the area she lived in, fully anticipating he would ask for updates, but he didn't. Draco was obviously one of those people with a built-in sat nav. He was one street away from the building where Eve lived before he asked for further directions.

'It's the next turn...you just went past it. Our

street lights are part of the council cuts,' she said by way of apology as he backed up.

She unfastened her seat belt, unable to conceal her palpable relief that her journey was at an end, though now it was she was able to concede she might have been overreacting. Alpha males were really not her thing; their earlier kiss was not her thing; nothing that had happened today was her thing.

Tomorrow happily was another day, a new start, a clean slate. Running out of clichés, she turned to Draco.

'Well, thank you.' Just to keep things unambiguous, she added, 'For the lift.' The kiss was something she would not forgive, but she had every intention of forgetting it or at least mentally filing it under *of no importance*.

'I'll see you in.'

She struggled to sound amused by the offer and reached for the door handle. 'That really won't be necessary. I can look after myself…see, I have my key…' Her hand came up empty from the pocket in her handbag where she always kept her key ring. 'It has to be in here somewhere…'

Several minutes later the contents of her bag had

been removed twice and replaced and it became clear that her keys might well be somewhere but they were definitely not in her bag.

'You lost your keys…it happens.'

His soothing words did not soothe.

'Not to me! I always… I had them when I was opening the car bonnet…' She summoned a mental image of the keys on their Tempting Eve logo fob. She covered her face with her hands and groaned. 'Oh, God, I left them in the ignition!'

'It's only keys.'

Her hands fell and she slung him a look. 'You're not the one locked out.'

'You have some spares, a neighbour with a key…?'

'Yes, but…' She shook her head. 'They have a baby and James works nights.' She shook her head positively. 'I can't knock up Sue and the baby at this time of night.' The last time she had seen her neighbour she had been shocked by her appearance.

Seeing her expression, Sue had grimaced, smoothed her hair self-consciously and said, 'Sleep deprivation is what they don't tell you about in antenatal classes.'

Eve couldn't believe it; she had crammed a lot of low moments into this day and he had been there to witness them all.

'Do you mind dropping me at a hotel?' She snapped open the mirror of her compact and closed it again without looking at it before sliding it back into her bag. There were some things it was just better not to know and how she looked at that moment was probably one of them!

Beneath the thin veneer of cheerful bravado she had clearly reached the end of her tether. Draco looked at her in thoughtful silence, tempted to do what she requested, and why not? She wasn't his responsibility and she had more in common with a feral cat than a needy kitten. Granted she'd had a hell of a day and it showed, but his hadn't been so great either—with a couple of memorable exceptions!

The internal tug of war was short-lived, and in the end his conscience won out, or was that his libido…?

'I know I've been a nuisance.'

He flashed a sideways glance her way. She looked dead on her feet, and he stifled a trickle of sympathy, killing it dead. 'Yes.' Without a word he started the engine.

Eve compressed her lips, feeling considerably less guilty. Charm really was his middle name! After the key debacle she surreptitiously checked her purse to make sure she had her credit cards, and she struggled against the temptation to check again. He already thought she was a total head case, so why confirm it for him?

Happily the journey back to London didn't take long driving in this powerful car, and Draco showed no inclination to make conversation, which was a mercy. She glanced periodically at his profile, responding to some sort of compulsion that she chose not to analyse; it was remote, his expression stony.

She didn't recognise the area they ended up in, a quiet and ultra-exclusive backwater. The building he drew up outside with its Georgian portico overlooked a green square. A place like this was bound to be expensive, but she was past caring.

'Great.' Eve unclipped her seat belt. 'I'm sorry to put you to so much trouble—' she began formally, then stopped. She was talking to an empty space.

Draco got out of the car before the tension building in him cracked his jaw. The cynic in him
wanted to believe that she knew what all those
hungry little sideways glances were doing to him
but he knew that she didn't. The woman had no
wiles whatsoever, which made her more dangerous. Not exactly scientific, but it worked for
him and it explained the fact he was struggling
to keep his normal iron control in check—she
simply didn't slot into any of the categories that
women usually did.

She caught him up halfway up the steps to the
impressive entrance of the hotel. It wasn't until
she saw him insert a key into the door that the
penny dropped.

'This isn't a hotel.'

A ghost of a smile twitched his lips as he looked
down at her, his height advantage even more pro-
nounced than usual because of the step he stood
on.

'I love a bit of intellectual debate as much as the
next man but it's late, I'm tired and you look…'
his glance swept upwards from her feet until it
stilled on her heart-shaped face, the light sprinkling of freckles across the bridge of her narrow

nose standing out stark against the pallor of exhaustion that tinged her skin '...terrible.'

'You don't look so hot yourself.' The retort had sounded cold and cutting in her head but it emerged sounding petty and childish.

It was also a big fat lie. The visible dark shadow on his face and the spikiness of his hair caused by his habit of running his hand back and forth across his dark head when he was exasperated did not detract in the least from his sinful attractiveness.

Her glance drifted to his hand on the door. He had nice hands, she mused, big and strong with long, tapering fingers. She averted her eyes but the heat continued to spread through her body. There was no way in the world she was entering that house.

'It's been a long day.'

'I don't see the connection between the way I look and you not taking me to a hotel.'

'I assumed, wrongly it would seem, that this would be more convenient for you.'

'So you made the unilateral decision and expected me to go along with it.' Staying the night under his roof filled her with a panic that was irrational. It wasn't as if he was going to demand her body in payment for bed and board. 'Call me a cab!' she demanded, panic making her sound imperious.

His eyes narrowed. Draco was sick of humouring her. 'Madre di Dio!' he gritted through clenched teeth.

Eve stared, her startled green eyes round. His accent was so perfect that she'd almost forgotten he wasn't British, but right at that moment his Latin heritage was pretty hard to miss, as the combustible quality she had sensed he possessed under the surface had smouldered into life—and it was pretty impressive.

'Suit yourself! Spend a night in a hotel room without so much as a toothbrush but spare me the histrionics and call your own damned cab!'

'I will!' She watched him step into the hallway and without warning her annoyance melted as the sense of guilt she had morphed into embarrassed contrition as she saw the day through his eyes. Images of herself flitted through her head; she really hadn't covered herself in glory today.

As first impressions went, chucking her bag of lingerie samples over him took the biscuit. Then sobbing all over him in the ladies' room, telling him God knew what; she really didn't want to remember. And then she'd turned what was meant to be a face-saving kiss into some sort of marathon kissing competition. Just when he'd probably thought it was all over, he'd had to rescue her from wandering around alone in the depths of the Surrey countryside. Taking a deep breath, she followed him inside.

'Sorry, you're right. I'm not that woman.' It suddenly seemed important that he know this.

'What woman?'

'The one I've been today. I don't usually do girly crying, I don't normally need rescuing and I can call my own cabs.'

'Can you also perhaps resist the temptation to cut off your nose to spite your face?'

Following a short silence and an internal debate to which he was not privy, she nodded. 'Thank you. I would be grateful of a bed for the night.' There had to be a dozen or so to spare. The place, if the hallway they stood in was any indicator, was enormous. Typically Georgian, very light, with a really beautiful staircase rising up all three floors.

'If it's not too much trouble for...?'

He watched as she looked around as though she expected an army of servants to materialise.

'Just us tonight. What's wrong? Are you afraid of being alone with me?'

'Don't be stupid.' If she had an ounce of sense she would be. If she had an ounce of sense she wouldn't be here at all; she'd be in a hotel room. Instead she had capitulated far too easily to his suggestion that she stay here—well, more than suggestion, really; he had presented it as a *fait accompli*.

Eve wished she were surer of her own motives but she had a feeling that at some level her impulsive choice to stay had more to do with her hormones than any practical reasons.

The memory of the hunger that had devoured her when they had kissed terrified her, but it also drew her and she had a horrible feeling that he knew it.

His attitude had been take it or leave it, but underneath all that did he think they'd end up sharing a bed tonight?

Do you, Eve?

She pushed away the thought. 'I just thought that someone might be waiting up for you?'

The idea seemed to amuse him. 'We have no live-in servants.'

'So nobody like my mother, you mean?' she fired back.

'Like...?' he echoed with a shrug. 'I don't know your mother and I wouldn't dream of judging anyone by what they do.'

She flushed at the reprimand. 'Well, that makes you unique, or maybe you like to think of yourself as egalitarian but if your daughter announced she was marrying the boy who stacks the shelves in the local supermarket you wouldn't be so tolerant, I suspect.'

'My daughter is thirteen. I wouldn't be happy if she said she was marrying Prince Harry. I'm curious—are you really such a cynic or is it that chip on your pretty shoulder showing again?' As he spoke he opened a panelled door to his right and after a short angry pause she accepted the silent invitation and walked past him.

The room they entered was not enormous. There was an original Adam fireplace filled with unlit candles, some nice artwork on the walls, and the furniture was an eclectic mix of expensive modern pieces and original Georgian antiques.

It was simple and uncomplicated, unlike the man who lived here.

Her covert gaze slid to Draco, who had walked straight over to a bureau and pulled out a bottle and a glass.

'I like to keep it simple. Mrs Ellis, the house-keeper, is full time, but she doesn't live in and she oversees the girls who come in, and my driver is—'

'I get the picture—simple.'

He poured himself a second finger of brandy and downed it in one gulp. 'Sorry, nightcap?'

She nodded. 'Please, thank you. You have a beautiful home. Have you lived here long?'

'Since last year. Before that I split my time pretty much fifty, fifty between here and Italy, but my sister's married a Brit and her daughter, Kate, is Josie's age. When I was looking for a school for Josie she recommended the one Kate attends.' He arched a brow. 'You don't want to know any of that, do you? What you're really thinking is, is he going to make a pass at me?'

She flushed to the roots of her hair and took a large sip of the brandy.

'Whereas I'm standing here thinking, is she going to make a pass at me?'

Her squeaked protest drew his lazy grin. 'You see—it's not so nice to have someone look at you as though they expect you to leap on them any minute, is it?'

She held the glass in both hands and looked at him over the rim. Her eyes watered as the brandy stung her throat and pooled with a warm glow in her stomach. 'You have a very weird mind.'

'And you have a very good body, and for a designer your dress sense is...*interesting.*'

An insult and a compliment. Which should she respond to? In the end she chose neither. 'It's late, so if you don't mind...?'

'I'll show you the way.'

Like everything else in the place the doorway was generous but even so Eve found herself hunching her shoulders to make herself smaller as she went through, as though touching him would ignite some invisible touch paper. Annoyed at herself, in the hallway she lifted her head and pulled her shoulders back. She was acting as though she were a victim of her own hormones; his touch would not release some sort of carnal chain reaction unless she allowed it to.

She followed him up the deep curving staircase, her heart beating, her emotions see-sawing.

He reached the upper hallway and, without turning, pointed to his right. 'I'm up that way. The guest suites are that way—take your pick. Except probably the last two. Clare uses the end one when she stays over and my mother leaves a few things in the one next to it.'

He caught her look and said, 'Clare is my ex-wife.'

An ex-wife who slept over: very civilised… Just how civilised, exactly? she wondered.

'No, we don't have sex.'

Her eyes widened at this fresh evidence of his ability to read her mind.

CHAPTER SEVEN

'RELAX, I'M NOT a mind-reader, you're just incredibly transparent and in answer to that thought nothing is going to happen between us tonight. Unless you want it to...?'

Eve recognised it was a taunt, not an invitation, but if it had been?

The question formed before she could stop it and dangerous thoughts swirled in her head. She felt caught between anger and... She shook her head, refusing to recognise that sensation in the pit of her stomach as excitement. The admission would open too many doors she didn't want to look behind.

'You said before you were not that woman, the one who cries and needs a shoulder, the one who gets rescued, that isn't you.'

She shook her head, wary of walking into some sort of trap. 'No.'

'So tell me, what *is* you?'

Eve looked away, avoiding his disturbingly intent stare, her negligent shrug masking her confusion. Before today she could have replied to that question with total confidence, but today had challenged a lot of things she'd previously taken as given and now wasn't the moment to think about them. She had to stay focused.

On what?

She felt a cold finger of unease trace a path up along her spine. She was only one stumbling step away from panic; she had always known her aim and gone for it… It gave her purpose, stability.

She tilted her head back to look at him, releasing a sigh of relief as, no longer treading water, she felt her feet touch bottom. 'I am…sensible.'

She half expected him to laugh but he didn't. 'And is it fun being sensible?'

She was fully prepared to defend undervalued common sense, but as her glance locked with his dark eyes framed by those crazily long silky eyelashes she experienced a stab of breath-snatching, heart-racing lust. It was followed by an equally fierce flash of anger that made her lash out.

'I think your idea of fun and mine is very different.'

Draco genuinely didn't give a damn what people thought about him, which had proved an advantage over the years. Losing his temper was a distraction that he did not normally allow himself.

He did not react to insults, it was a mindset and usually it was not a struggle for him to keep his cool, but Eve's lip-curling contempt touched an exposed nerve and his temper spiked.

'Oh, I think we might find we have some common ground, *cara*.' He opened the mental door he had shut them behind and allowed the memories to come flooding in. Her small, eager hands skating over his skin, her nails digging in, the frantic little moans as she had kissed him sent a hard throb of lust slamming through his body, the strength of it making him catch his breath.

A threat disguised as an invitation or an invitation disguised as a threat? It didn't really matter to Eve. What mattered was her body's response.

It was sheer bloody-minded defiance that stopped her retreating as he took a step towards her radiating anger and arrogance and sheer *maleness*. Such a suggestion a short time ago would have evoked a scornful response; now it sent an illicit thrill surging through Eve's body. She licked her lips and tasted brandy, but the buzz in her head had nothing to do with the alcohol. His dark, predatory stare was more potent and more mind-destroying than an entire bottle of liquor!

He saw her pupils dilate, the dark centre swallowing up all but a thin rim of green, and gave a hard smile of satisfaction.

Common sense, she called it. He called it pragmatism and he could do with some now to counteract the lust throbbing through his body. There were warning bells—there had been warning bells since the moment he first saw her.

He'd spent the day ignoring them and as he reached out to curve a hand around the back of her head he carried on doing so, thinking instead about her lush mouth. He couldn't remember the last time he had wanted a woman this much...the last time he had burned this way.

It was a kind of insanity... He thought he would go insane if he didn't have her, but she wanted him too; he could see it in the flush on her skin, the tremor in the hand she raised in a fluttery gesture to her lips and then let drop.

But most of all it was in her eyes, her *hungry* eyes, so deep he could have drowned in them.

He slid his fingers into her silky hair meeting a barrier of pins. He removed one and let it fall to the floor, and then another.

Her eyes widened in alarm then half closed. A silent sigh left her parted lips as she breathed in and out fast and shallow, focusing on the mechanics of it, as if drawing air into her lungs and releasing it and not the fact she was floating on a sensual cloud several inches above the floor was the most important thing.

'I'm not having sex with you.' It was hard to force the words out with her tongue stuck to the roof of her mouth, but it needed saying as much for her benefit as his. When she did finally have sex it would be with a man she felt comfortable with, a man she could—

'Good to know,' he slurred thickly. 'But this is okay...' He stroked a finger softly over the skin around her ear. 'Right?'

It felt so right it hurt.

She struggled to retrieve her previous thought: a man she could...? *Control.* She shook her head slightly and found her cheek against his palm as she thought, That sounds wrong.

She genuinely didn't want to control this fu-

ture lover; no, she just wanted to be *in* control...
Draco found another pin and a deep visceral shudder stronger than the rest shook her, making her
body vibrate like a tuning fork.

In control like now, mocked the voice in her
head.

She squeezed her eyes closed in an effort to
close down the thoughts and felt the touch of his
lips on her eyelids light as a breeze.

Hands framing her face, he lifted his eyes and
watched as her hair succumbed to gravity and the
weight of the shiny coils slid downwards in slow
motion to settle against her narrow back.

His hissing breath caused her eyes to open. Her
eyelids felt heavy, but she felt light, as though she
were floating; it was surreal.

'This feels really strange.'

He bared his teeth in a smile that made her
shiver. 'It's meant to feel good.'

She swallowed and, eyes huge on his face, whispered thickly, 'It d-does.'

'Sexy stutter.'

Stutters weren't sexy, but she let the comment
stand; it was more empowering than she would

have believed possible to have this gorgeous man telling her she was sexy.

Again he replied as though she'd voiced her doubts. 'It is sexy.'

He kissed her then, slowly, deeply, his hands framing her face, his long fingers stroking her scalp. Her lips parted under the pressure and he sank deep into her mouth, taking his time, drinking her in, savouring the taste of her. The possessive thrust of his tongue made the heat that had been slowly building inside her spark and explode like a firework display.

She wanted him more than she had wanted anything in her life. Blinded by sheer need, her control a thing of the past, Eve reached for him, rising up on her toes.

This is so not you, Eve.

The voice in her head was wrong because it *was* her and they *were* her fingers wrapping themselves into the fabric of his shirt and she was the one kissing him back with a wildness and ferocity that he answered with equally wild, head-spinning passion. He wrapped one hand in her hair, the other, like an iron band, he placed around her waist, lifting her off the ground as he plunged his tongue deeper into her mouth, drawing a soft mewling cry from her throat as he withdrew and repeated the process.

She was barely conscious that they had been moving all the time, moving, walking, stumbling, kissing, his mouth on hers, his lips moving, his hands on her body sliding over fabric, under fabric, over skin, everything fuelling the wild desperation that pounded through Eve. The only thing stopping her from falling as she blindly allowed herself to be steered down the wide hallways was her grip on the fabric of his shirt at waist level. There was no underlying softness to grab as his belly was corrugated with hard muscle. When they hit a pedestal displaying a Chinese urn, the piece of porcelain went flying.

'No!' A finger on her cheek stopped her turning her head towards the smashing sound. 'It's nothing,' he rasped, desperate not to break the mood. She stared up at him, the urgency in his voice echoed in the starkly beautiful, strained lines of his face and the molten heat burning in his heavy-lidded, half-closed eyes.

She stopped thinking about broken china; she forgot thinking about everything except the here and now. Her entire world was here, his face, his heat, and if the ceiling had fallen on their heads she wouldn't have noticed. She'd have just carried on looking and wanting.

She wanted to touch him, taste him… She was quivering with need, shaking from head to toe.

The grip of fingers in her hair was tight but not as tight as the grip of his dark, glowing stare.

'It's fine…' he murmured as his nose brushed along the side of hers. The gentle nip at the soft curve of the trembling fullness of her lower lip sent her deeper into the sensual maelstrom that held her enthralled.

'I love your mouth.' His tongue traced the outline until she widened her mouth, inviting him to deepen his erotic invasion.

They had reached his bedroom door when the buttons of his shirt gave way under the pressure of her purchase and Eve stumbled, but before she lost her balance he was able to scoop her up and carry her into the bedroom.

His impatient kick set the door hard against the wall but he didn't register the framed landscape on the wall vibrating hard enough to crack the glass as he closed it with his foot.

He walked across to the bed and, pulling back the quilt to reveal crisp white sheets, he placed her on the cool silk.

Eve pulled herself into a kneeling position, her glorious hair tumbled about her flushed face and her emerald eyes glazed with passion. She looked so totally gorgeous that it took all his will power to resist the primal need to simply sink into her and feel her close around him, but her pleasure was as important for Draco's satisfaction as his own and he needed to be sure she was ready for him.

Instead he left the moisture from a slow trail of kisses he pressed to her throat and straightened up.

Kneeling there on the big bed, struggling to breathe past the tangled knot of emotion in her chest, she watched as he rid himself of his shirt.

A hot breath snagged in her throat. She wanted him, and how could anything that felt so good be wrong? A hundred examples came to mind and she brushed them all away with fierce determination and caught hold of the unfastened ends of the belt that dangled from his belt loops.

He smiled as she tugged, not resisting the pressure that brought him to the edge of the bed where she knelt. Eve continued to gaze up at him; he was so perfect he made her ache.

Eve stared up at him with a mixture of fascination, awe and hunger. She had never seen anything so beautiful. There was not an ounce of spare flesh to blur the perfect definition of each individual muscle, and with his flat belly and broad powerful chest he made her think of a classical sculpture, but his skin was not stone, it was deep gold.

He slid the belt she had held out of its loops and let it drop to the floor but left his trousers hanging low over his slim hips as he took her wrists.

'I'm going to undress you now.'

She felt a spasm of uncertainty, but quashed it. This man could have any woman he wanted and he clearly wanted her. She wasn't even sure he saw her nod.

She sat there fighting to breathe and trembling as he took hold of the hem of her top and lifted it over her head, letting it fall to the floor. She had nothing but a thin camisole on under it.

'Look at me, Eve.'

When she didn't he sank down onto his knees on the bed beside her and, taking her chin in his hand, forced her face up to his. 'You are beautiful.'

She quivered as his hand cupped one breast, his thumb rubbing across the turgid peak that protruded through the thin fabric. The sensation, along with the expression in his eyes, blasted all her uncertainties away.

She responded to the pressure of his hand on her breastbone and fell back on the pile of pillows. With an impatient grunt he pulled them out from under her head until she lay flat with him over her. They kissed, deep, soul-piercing kisses that left her aching and wanting more, so much more.

'You shall have it. You shall have everything, *cara*,' he promised thickly. 'First we do not need these.'

She lay there as he skilfully removed the rest of her clothing, exposing her to his hungry, burning gaze, and wondered if she had spoken out loud or had he read her mind again?

Very soon it no longer seemed to matter. But as they kissed and he caressed her until every cell in her body was on fire Eve learnt there were benefits to having a man who knew what you wanted before you did!

When she had reached a point where she was one ache, he levered himself up into a kneeling position and slid down the zip on his trousers, holding her eyes and only breaking contact to slide them down his long legs, his boxers swiftly following.

'Oh, mercy!'

He laughed and touched the corner of her mouth with his thumb, then met her lips with his, drinking in her sweet flavour, savouring the taste, the erotic movement of her tongue against his.

'I want to taste all of you.'

His voice was like smoke as it clung; it seeped into every corner of her. Above it was the thunderous clamour of her heart.

'Relax, enjoy it, *cara*,' he whispered in her ear.

The intimacy of his touch, the audacious and shockingly effective caresses of his mouth and tongue should have shocked her virginal sensibilities, but Eve felt only pleasure as she moved against his hand and his mouth, letting him drive her to the edge again and again.

As her hand closed around the hard, silky thickness of his shaft he gasped and groaned. 'I have to have you, Eve, now.'

She opened her legs in silent invitation and when he moved over her, she lifted her hips to open herself for him. The first deep thrust took her breath away but as he started to move she realised there was more…and with each successive measured thrust of his hips he drove her deeper and deeper into the heart of the heat that burned inside her, until she was the heat.

The climax when it hit her was so intense that her cry rivalled the feral moan that emanated from his chest.

CHAPTER EIGHT

'WHAT ARE YOU DOING?'

Eve glanced towards the bed and immediately regretted it as he was looking magnificently rumpled. 'Getting dressed,' she mumbled.

'So why are you wrapped in the duvet?'

'Because I'm cold.' She would be after a cold shower.

'Right, because for a minute there I thought you might be going coy on me.'

She felt the embarrassed heat climb to her cheeks. Draco was right: it was absurd. He had got out of bed stark naked earlier and been totally relaxed, but the idea of him seeing her naked in daylight had sent her under the duvet. 'Don't be stupid,' she scorned.

'Considering there is not an inch of your body I have not explored...of course if I missed anywhere...'

He hadn't; he had even kissed the small fresh

scar from the mole removal and told her they both had one. His, she had learnt, was from a skiing accident. She had kissed it too… She pushed the memory away, but she couldn't push away the warmth that remained low in her pelvis.

'Look, last night happened and I'm not trying to pretend it didn't,' she said. The second time they had made love had been even more intense than the first as he had encouraged her to explore his body while he had tutored her in how to please him in a voice that embodied sin. 'But—'

'You regret it?' His tone was sharp.

'No, but today is another day.'

He loosed a long whistle through his teeth 'Wow, now that really *is* profound.'

Responding to his aggravating sarcasm—*only aggravating if you let him get to you, Eve*—she turned her head sharply, intending to deliver an acid response. At the same moment, like a lazy big cat, he stretched. Disastrously distracted by the ripple of taut muscle in his ribbed belly and perfectly defined chest, she almost dropped the quilt.

'You still haven't explained how I'm your first lover.' How a woman who was as innately sen-

sual as Eve had reached this point without having taken a man to her bed defied logic and his
powers of deduction, but he wasn't going to com-
plain as it was to his benefit. 'Did it not occur to
you that it is the sort of thing a man might like to
know upfront?'

'I didn't think you'd notice.' Keeping one hand
on the quilt, she stalked back to the bed. 'What's
so funny?'

He looped his hands behind his neck, drawing
her eyes back to the muscles of his lean torso.
'You are...'

Her scowl refused to stay in place, he was so
incredibly gorgeous.

'But deflections aside—'

'I was not trying to deflect anything.'

'It's a simple question, Eve.' He grabbed her arm
and Eve sat down on the bed. 'Better,' he murmured, easing closer until their faces were close.
'Nobody is a virgin at your age by accident.' He
tugged the quilt, holding her eyes as it slid down
to her waist.

'I've not had time for r-romance.'

'Last night wasn't romance, it was sex, Eve.'
The best sex he had ever had.

She lowered her chin to hide the hurt anger she knew was written on her face. When she lifted it again she was smiling. 'You really don't have to spell it out to me, Draco. I hardly thought it was the start of a deep and meaningful relationship.'

Her laugh grated on him. Her entire attitude grated on him; it wasn't as though he was looking for deep and meaningful any more than he'd been looking for a virgin to take to his bed. A virgin…! Eyes half closed, he relived that moment when he had known…and felt again the equally powerful surge of possessiveness that had been too primal to deny and still was—he was her first.

'You're a passionate woman, Eve.'

She shook her head, not able to admit even to herself her secret fear of losing control with a man, that she might lose some of herself at the same time… Her eyes lifted, a furrow appearing between her brows as she wondered what it was about him that made it all right to lose control.

'I've been b-building a b-business.'

His dark brows lifted. 'That is a reason?'

She nodded.

'It is possible to have sex and run a business at the same time, I promise you, *cara.*'

'I don't want a full-time relationship and I'm not into one-night stands.' A bit late to remember that, Eve. 'And even if I was in the market, men who share my aims and ambitions are hard to find.'

'There is nothing stopping you looking for one of them while you have sex with me. But, believe me, one night with you would not be nearly enough for any man, *cara*. Actually,' he mused, smiling to himself at the blush that had spread to all parts of her body, 'I think you'll find you can go to bed with a man who shares your aims and ambitions and wake up with a man who is not even faintly interested in your mind… Most men will say anything to get you into bed.'

'But you're different, I suppose?'

'As a matter of fact I am. I am exactly the sort of man you need.'

'Is that meant to be a turn-on?' Eve had no idea if this arrogant pronouncement was intended to arouse her, but it did.

'Think about it. I can give you great sex—and it was great—with no strings, no emotional upheaval, just satisfying sex. You may have no time in your calendar for romance, but I think a clever girl like you could fit in great sex.'

'That sounds…'

'Perfect?'

'Immoral!'

His husky laughter rang out. 'Stay with me long enough, angel, and I will corrupt you; you do have a body made for sin.'

Dropping the quilt, she rose from the bed, swept her clothes up into a bundle and marched into the bathroom.

As the door closed on her beautifully rounded little bottom he gave a loud groan. There were in his experience few certainties in life, but he found himself faced with one total certainty: he had to get Eve back in his bed or die trying.

Eve always arrived at the office first. She enjoyed those few minutes alone with no interruptions to plan out her day and get her thoughts together. Today she had arrived when her assistant was already at her desk with sympathy, a herbal tea she said always worked for jet lag and a wistful expression she always wore when she talked about weddings.

Eve accepted the sachet of tea and told Shelley she hadn't taken any photos.

'None?' The girl couldn't hide her disappointment. 'I suppose you were too stressed about today to enjoy yourself and let your hair down.'

Eve lifted a hand to her head just to satisfy herself it was neatly subdued. Unlike her imagination. *Just glorious; I want to wrap myself in your hair...* The flashback, the throaty, sinfully sexy voice was so real she could almost feel his warm breath on her neck.

Swallowing, she lowered her eyes, willing the flush to stay below neck level as her fingers tightened hard enough around the herbal sachet to make the contents spill out.

'I'll just...' She took a step towards her office then stopped, a frown pleating her smooth brow as she turned back. *'Today?'*

Her assistant blinked and brought up a chart on her tablet. 'There hasn't been *another* delay, has there? They are still letting you know this morning...?'

Eve struggled to conceal her dismay behind a cheerful smile that made her face ache. She had a point to make or at least a reputation to preserve—a reputation for being calm and unflappable in a crisis.

'No, it's still this morning.'

Inside the office she closed the door and leaned against it. This was not just a disaster, it was a… What the hell was it?

She had forgotten!

How could she have forgotten?

For six months her every waking moment had been focused on this deal; she had invested all her time and energy on it; she had lived and breathed it, focused on a goal and gone for it. She told herself that failure was not an option but she knew it always was, and that knowledge had made her wake up in a cold sweat in the middle of the night on more than one occasion.

And now on the very brink, she glanced down at her watch, and then lifted a hand to her face in shock. Within minutes she'd be receiving that crucial decision and she'd completely forgotten about it!

What did they say? Pride came before a fall… She had gone back to her flat that morning to change feeling pretty smug. Well, actually more *relieved*. Eve knew she wasn't like her mother or any of the other women she knew who lost the capacity to be objective when there was a man in their bed, but there had been a niggling doubt—what if great sex stole her self-respect and made her willing to compromise all her principles?

Well, she'd had great sex; to her shock, the sort of mind-bending, head-banging sex that she'd had really did exist outside novels! Her body still ached from it—in a good way—and for a short time she'd stopped being the Queen of Caution and allowed her impulses full rein. It had turned out to be a totally liberating experience. Draco was an incredible lover but equally importantly in the cold light of day he was still an arrogant pain in the neck, which might for all she knew be what made him a great lover; the point was, she knew he was. She wasn't making excuses for his shortcomings; she wasn't about to put him on a pedestal or keep her mouth shut when she knew he was wrong.

It was a relief to have her theory confirmed. It wasn't sex that turned women into willing slaves; it was love. She didn't love Draco, and the very idea of falling in love after twenty-four hours made her lips twitch into a fleeting ghost of a smile.

Love... To be honest, she didn't even like

him that much. If she never saw him again, she wouldn't lose any sleep. That was why in some ways he was right. He was perfect as a lover—there was nothing between them but unbridled lust, nothing complicated by emotions. It had just been sex—very good sex, to be sure—but there were a lot of men out there who were not Draco, men whose hands weren't so skilful perhaps…

An image of his long fingers gliding over her skin drifted into Eve's head, igniting heat low in her pelvis until she pushed the image away and reminded herself that she was in no hurry to repeat their night of passion. Another uncomplicated moment might happen but she was not going out looking for it.

Uncomplicated or not, the unwelcome fact remained that a night spent with him had knocked the contract that she'd worked so hard for completely out of her head…

Maybe I'm the exception that proves the rule—the woman who can't multitask.

It's business success or sex; I can't do both.

Failing to summon a smile at her humour and not willing to acknowledge she was uncertain on this unfamiliar ground, Eve took a seat at her desk. She released a deep sigh, but the calm that the minimalist arrangement usually inspired, with no photos or personal items cluttering her working space, just the essentials, failed to materialise. She touched the row of pencils, taking comfort from the symmetry.

She needed to clear her head and focus.

Before she could do either, the phone bleeped and that was it. She gritted her teeth and lifted it, trying not to think of the people who had told her that she was running before she could walk.

Ten minutes later she replaced it.

She was shaking.

The deal was closed, and it was only now she could admit that there had been moments, though she had never said it out loud, when she had doubted the wisdom of her Australian trip. But the groundwork had paid off, and the exclusive department store chain with outlets all over the southern hemisphere was going to take her line.

This was the moment she had been working towards, pushing herself towards, the moment she had dreamed about.

A tiny furrow appeared between her brows. So where was the high…the euphoria…the glow of achievement? Instead it was almost an anticlimax, but that, she told herself, was only to be expected. To be really appreciated this was the sort of good news that deserved to be shared, and a line in Charlie Latimer's wedding speech came back to her: *Success means nothing unless you have someone to share it with—I have the best person in the world: my wife.*

Eve had not tasted the wine in her glass or joined in with the spontaneous ripple of applause and her eyes had remained dry but, his insincerity aside, didn't he have a point?

Who would be happy for her? Her mother was on her honeymoon and her best friend was busy being a pregnant princess.

She pushed away the sudden sharp stab of something she refused to recognise as self-pity, and thought, Buy a cat, Eve.

Or take a new lover.

There was still some mileage in the one she had, she thought wryly...or did she still have him? The situation was so far out of her comfort zone that she was still feeling her way...*all over his warm satiny textured skin.*

She looked down and saw her fingers stroking the desk. The dreamy expression clouding her eyes vanished and the furrow between her brows twitched back into life as a comment Draco had made came back to her.

She had no idea what time it had been when she'd woken, not in her own bed, but in a strange bed held down by the weight of a man's thigh thrown across her hips, his head between her breasts. The initial adrenaline-fed panic surge had made her struggle for a split second but then she'd realised where she was and relaxed against his warm chest.

He'd unconsciously voiced her inner doubts out loud. *What are you doing? Stop analysing—just enjoy. There's no tomorrow, just here and now, you and me. I don't want you to reach me emotionally. I just want you to touch me...please.*

The tortured plea had made her feel empowered, hot and out of control.

She laughed softly as she got to her feet. She wasn't even a little jealous of her friend; the last thing she wanted was a baby. She was far too busy with her career right now, but perhaps in a few years' time...? Her body clock had barely started ticking and she'd only just discovered sex.

She straightened the row of pencils on her desk one last time and, humming softly under her breath, headed for the interconnecting door to her PA's office. Shelley had really put in the extra hours on this one; actually, not just her PA, but everyone had, and though friends and family would say well done it was only the small team who really understood what this success meant to her.

Perhaps, she mused, she could take them for lunch at that new Italian everyone was raving about. Her stomach growled at the thought of food—toast and cereal had not been on the breakfast menu this morning and she had refused to sample what was!

'How do you feel about Italian, Shelley?' Eve asked as she opened the door to the outer office. She was used to the terrible clutter on the younger girl's desk but this was the first time she had found a man there.

And the man was Draco. His back was to her but there was no mistaking the identity of the tall figure who sat casually there. Him being here like this was wrong on so many levels.

'Steady!'

She was conscious of him unfolding his long

length from the desk and then towering over her as she struggled to regain first her balance and then her composure. She grabbed hold of it in both hands and enclosed herself in a shell of rigid formality.

Shell or not, it didn't protect her from the waves of whatever it was he exuded, and her jangling nerves made civility impossible. 'What the hell are you doing here, Draco?'

She sensed rather than saw her PA's wide eyes.

'There, didn't I tell you she'd be delighted to see me, Shelley Ann?'

Her assistant laughed, not her usual raucous giggle but a low sexy chuckle. The woman had a boyfriend whom she said she adored, so what was she doing? Eve slung her an exasperated look. Shelley could not be more obvious had she been salivating—but for Eve's interruption she'd probably be ripping off her top and screaming *Take me!*

Eve's generous lips tightened. She was all for women taking the initiative but there was such a thing as too eager. Not that she expected this view to be shared by a man like Draco. Her eyes made a scornful sweep over the tall, lean figure now propped casually back against the end of the desk. She had no doubt he enjoyed having women fawn all over him—in fact, he probably expected it and she was one in a long line of those who had helped build his belief in his irresistibility.

'I came to take you to lunch.' One corner of his mouth curled up in a slow intimate smile as his warm brown eyes moved over her face.

'How did you know where to find me?'

He produced a gilt-edged business card. 'You left it behind.' And the smell of her perfume.

Eve swallowed and hissed under her breath. 'I'm busy.'

'Actually the supplier emailed to cancel your meeting.'

'Thank you, Shelley Ann.' His smile made the younger girl blush and thrust out her not inconsiderable chest. 'So, you see, you're free, *cara*.'

Instead of asking him just what he was playing at Eve found her eyes drawn to his mouth. Free was the last thing she felt; she felt *compelled*! Willing her heart to slow, Eve brought her lashes down in a protective curtain.

'Did I hear you say that you liked Italian?' he asked.

'She adores Italian,' the younger girl cut back.

Eve winced, her jaw clenched, embarrassed for her assistant. 'It's not my favourite,' she lied.

'She loves it.'

Eve slung her another exasperated look and Shelley winked and directed a lascivious leer at Draco's back, mouthing an exaggerated, *He's gorgeous—go for it!*

I already did, Eve thought, and felt the colour staining her cheeks flame even brighter. 'I really am a little pushed for time today.'

He gave an exaggerated sigh and shrugged. 'Oh, well, if you can't make lunch, I suppose,' he conceded, 'we could discuss it here.'

Discuss...*it...?* Panic slid through Eve. Shelley was a great PA and totally discreet about work but when it came to less professional gossip...!

'Oh, no, take her to lunch.' Shelley pressed her palms together and rested her chin on her fingertips. Batting her eyes at Draco, she confided, 'It's her birthday.' She met her boss's glare with an innocent look. 'Well, he doesn't work here, does he?'

Thank God for small mercies!

'You said don't tell anyone in the *office*,' Shelley pointed out.

'Your birthday? Oh, well, that settles it,' Draco announced with satisfaction. 'I'm taking you to lunch.'

Eve would have loved to assure him that it settled nothing except the fact that he obviously couldn't comprehend a situation when a person wouldn't do what he wanted, but decided it was better to appear at least to give in gracefully than risk having her personal life discussed in front of an audience. The horror of this thought actually made her shudder.

Outside the building and away from the prying eyes of her assistant, Eve pulled away from the light touch of the hand he had placed between her shoulder blades as he guided her out of the building—as if she didn't know her own way.

'I am more than capable of—' She broke off, taking a sideways step to avoid being knocked over by a middle-aged man whose eyes were glued to his phone. Luckily the heavy line of traffic had ground to a standstill so all she did was step into a puddle, though Draco took the opportunity to haul her back to the pavement.

'We had sex.' Eve cleared her throat, privately congratulating herself on how matter of fact she had sounded when that statement sounded weird on so many levels.

He did not blink, just held her eyes with a stare that made her stomach muscles quiver with the same tension that shimmered in the air.

'I had not forgotten.' Though once he had felt her cool little hands on his skin he had forgotten almost everything else, but *that* he would never forget, if only for the reason Draco had never totally lost control with a woman before. He had always stayed in control of his passion, his lust. Ironically when he had lost it the woman who had disintegrated his control had been a virgin.

It turned out his initial suspicion regarding her innocence had been right after all. The shock had lessened but the sense of total mystification lingered. She was so sensual and so sweetly responsive that it made no sense she hadn't tried sex before, but the fact remained he was her first lover. In moments of honesty he admitted that he was not a worthy recipient of that gift, but in return he would teach her how to enjoy her own body.

Eve struggled to hold onto her antagonism. His deep voice had a tactile quality and his heavy-lidded stare did dangerous things to her as the busy street around them receded; it was scarily easy for the world to vanish when she looked into his eyes.

'That does not give you the right to stroll into my place of work and flirt with my staff.' Somehow her comment made it sound as though the latter was the worst sin. 'I don't suppose you can help yourself,' she muttered.

'Lighten up, Eve.'

She compressed her lips, irritated by his amused response. 'I'm perfectly *light*, thank you.'

His eyes widened as if in sudden comprehension. 'Or is it one of *those* birthdays,' he commiserated.

Her expression froze. 'I'm not thirty for ages yet.'

He grinned and chalked up an invisible point in the air. 'It's reassuring to know that you have some of the normal vanities.' His dark gaze grew warmer and more intent as he touched a finger to her chin, tilting her face up to his. 'You look about eighteen, which can be a little disconcerting, especially when half the time you act as though you're middle-aged.'

He gives and then he takes away she thought, snatching her chin from his grip and rubbing angrily with the heel of her hand at the tingling area of skin where there had been contact. 'You say the n-nicest things,' she said with an insincere smile.

'You do take life seriously.'

Her jaw tautened as she tossed back a scornful response. 'That's the difference between you and me; I think life *is* serious.'

He gave a tiny nod of acknowledgement. 'Life is also sad and funny…' He stopped as his car drew up beside them at the kerbside and, nodding to the driver, he opened the rear passenger door for Eve. As she got in he wondered why the hell he was discussing the meaning of life with this woman. He could have asked himself why he was here with her at all, but that question was more easily answered, though no less strange.

He wanted her, not in itself strange but the compulsive nature of it was. If he had thought about it too deeply Draco might have been troubled, but he didn't; he mentally categorised it as an appetite like any other, and like any man when it came to sex Draco enjoyed the pursuit.

But when was the last time he'd actually rear-ranged his schedule to pursue any woman…?

Dismissing the question, he reminded himself that, no matter how intense the attraction between them or how seemingly insatiable the hunger this woman aroused in him, history would inevitably repeat itself and he would lose interest. He was unable to exactly recall his sister's recent exasperated assessment of his love life, but he did remember that she'd likened him to a child in a sweet shop.

All that instant gratification, Draco, but one of these days, brother, you'll lose your taste for sugar and realise that what you need is something with a bit more bite.

'It's a matter of balance, *cara*,' he mused out loud as he slid into the limo beside her. 'The tough times in life are made bearable only if you don't waste the good ones.' He leaned forward and gave the driver instructions, speaking in Italian. The man, who was as big as a bear, replied in the same language.

'What self-help book did you get that little gem from or was it a Christmas cracker?'

'My father died unexpectedly, and it was devastating for those of us left behind, especially my mother, but the thing she clung to and still does is that there was not a single day in his life that he didn't live to the full. Not that he did spectacular things—it was the little things he took pleasure from, be it a great bottle of wine or his grandchild's first step.'

She was instantly remorseful for her snappy retort. 'Oh, I'm so sorry.'

'As my father would have said, bad stuff happens but until it does laugh a little.'

She shifted uneasily in her seat under the directness of his penetrating stare. 'I get the feeling that you don't laugh a lot, which is a shame as you have a nice laugh. It sounds like your hair feels on my skin… Speaking of which, do you put it up because you like me taking it down?'

She swallowed and lowered her gaze in confusion. All it took from him was a couple of husky-voiced compliments and her heart was tripping like a steam hammer. 'I p-put it up because it gets in the way.'

He leaned back in his seat, crossing one ankle over the other. 'And you like things neat.'

'Is that a crime?' she flared.

'Do you want to know what I think…?'

'No!' she blurted, leaning forward in her seat and shouting. 'We're here!' The man ignored her. She turned to round to face Draco. 'Is he deaf?'

'I think you mean hearing-impaired, *cara*, and he wasn't deaf, but after you yelled down his ear like that it's certainly possible. There is parking around the rear.'

'Oh. Sorry.'

The car pulled into one of the parking spaces Draco had referred to and came to a standstill. Draco said something in Italian to the driver, who laughed.

'Are you talking about me?' she asked suspiciously.

'Not everything is about you, *cara*. Do you *really* want to eat?'

Eve stared at him. 'Wasn't that the idea?'

He looked at her for a moment and then gave one of his inimitable shrugs. 'It is an option certainly.' This time when he spoke to the driver it was in English. 'Thank you, Carl, we'll get a cab back.'

The restaurant was busy; people were waiting for tables. Eve felt relief that there was absolutely no way they were going to get one.

CHAPTER NINE

FIVE MINUTES LATER they were being shown to their table by an attentive Italian waiter who at Draco's request conversed in English.

'In case you thought we were talking about you.'

'Very funny. Is that man really your driver...?'

Draco looked at her curiously. 'Carl...? What do you think he is?'

'A bodyguard?'

Draco's throaty laugh caused several heads to turn. She covered her glass with her hand. 'I'm working.'

'It's your birthday.'

The battle was short, as the constant bickering was tiring. It might be better, she decided, to save her energy for the important points...and anyway a glass of wine might help soothe her jangling nerves.

She tipped her head. 'All right, just a small one.' Actually there were worse ways to spend your birthday than sitting in a really good restaurant with a man whom every woman in the room had stared at when he walked in, though she imagined that the novelty would wear thin pretty quickly and it might even cause the odd jealous twinge to be with a man so universally lusted after. She angled a glance at his face. Was he *really* as oblivious as he seemed to all the lustful stares…?

'No, Carl is my driver.'

'So you don't have a bodyguard?' she probed, unable to hide her curiosity.

'The best sort of security is the sort people don't see.'

She put down her fork and leaned back in her seat, cradling her glass. 'That's not an answer.'

His response to her indignation was a slow, lazy grin. 'It is the only one I am giving.' He sat back in his chair and watched her make serious inroads into the rustic pasta dish she had chosen.

'This is really good.' Eve took another sip of her wine, determined to make it last. She glanced at his plate. 'Steak is a bit safe.' He had only eaten half of it. 'How did we get this table anyway?'

'I know the owner.'

She had suspected it must be something like that. 'The one who owns the entire chain?'

He nodded. 'That's right.'

'They're everywhere now but when I was in Paris last year it had just opened, and the place was heaving.'

She broke off as the manager approached.

'Sir...' he tipped his head to include Eve '...miss, I hope the meal was satisfactory?'

'It was delicious,' she said.

'We're happy customers,' Draco added.

There was something she couldn't *quite* put her finger on it, but the manager's manner when he spoke to Draco and Draco's manner when he replied...and then it came to her.

She waited until the older man had gone before testing her theory.

'Are you the owner?'

He didn't even blink. 'For the past two years.'

Her dark brows knitted as she straightened her cutlery, once, twice and then once more. She was bewildered by her inability to hold eye contact with him without feeling shivery and self-conscious.

'It didn't occur to you to mention it?'

'No.' Elbows set on the table, he leaned forward. 'So are you going home?'

'Home?'

'For your birthday.'

Eve retreated behind her wine glass. 'I have no home.'

'Boo-hoo! Wow, you really do have a chip on your shoulder, don't you?'

She responded to the callous charge angrily. 'I lived at Brent Manor for t-ten years but it was never my *home*, we were just the help.'

'Yet being the help, as you put it, did not prevent you and Hannah becoming friends and now your mother is the mistress of the house.'

Eve was not about to satisfy his curiosity, but he was not the first to remark on the unlikely upstairs, downstairs friendship. Hannah Latimer with money, charm and princess looks, who went to a prestigious private school and the painfully shy cook's daughter who went to school in the local town.

For Eve it had been hate at first sight and she had gone out of her way to avoid the daughter of the house with her golden hair and her permanent smile. She'd had numerous hiding places on the estate and when she'd found Hannah in one of those she'd initially been furious—until she'd seen the tears.

The girls had discovered they had something in common a long time before they'd found out their parents were having an affair. They'd both hated school and had both been bullied, although for different reasons.

'People find the entire rags to riches story fascinating…not literally rags, I know that, but don't be surprised if you find details of your mother's life popping up in gossip columns. We all have skeletons,' Draco warned.

She stiffened, horror seeping into her at the thought of her parentage becoming public knowledge, and retorted defensively, 'What are you implying?'

Draco realised immediately from her reaction that there was definitely a skeleton in the Curtis family closet. Hell, all he'd wanted to do was steer the conversation in the right direction… Oh, well, that left the direct approach.

'There is a photo that has been posted online. I thought you should know about it.'

He pushed his phone across the table and

watched her face as she looked at the explicit photo of the two of them in an abandoned embrace the night of the wedding. He saw the colour run up under her fair skin when she saw what it was, and then recede leaving her paper pale. 'One of your enterprising ex school friends I assume.'

Eve closed her eyes and for a long moment she said nothing. Then in a hopeful whisper said, 'Perhaps no one will see it.'

There was no gentle way to break it so he just said it. 'Sorry, but apparently it has already gone viral.'

She covered her mouth with her hand, and above it her green eyes registered total horror. How could he sound so calm?

'You have to stop them.' He shook his head and she added wildly, 'What if your daughter sees it?'

'The odds are she already has. On the plus side it is quite flattering.'

She closed her eyes. Flattering? Was he insane? She was an intensely private person and the idea of that photo out there made Eve... 'I feel sick.' She waited until the strong wave of nausea had passed before asking, 'So what are we going to do?'

He arched a brow. *'Do?'*

'A plan.'

'There is no plan beyond damage limitation. Take my word for it—I have been here before.'

'Well, I haven't!'

'My best advice is to laugh it off, or maintain a dignified silence...'

A hoarse laugh was shaken from her throat. She could see precious little dignity in having pictures of yourself in a passionate clinch posted on the internet. It wouldn't just be strangers who would see it, but people who knew her: her mother, her friends, people she worked with.

'Or I could deny vigorously that there is anything going on between us.'

She exhaled. 'Good.'

'Which will convince them that something definitely is and prolong the interest in us.'

Eve clenched her teeth, her body rigid as she fought the urge to rush around the table and shake him. She firmly believed that violence never solved anything but on this occasion it might make her feel a hell of a lot better!

He met her eyes. 'Tell me what you want me to do?'

'I don't kn-know,' she admitted miserably.

'Then shall I tell you what I want to do? I want to get up and leave this place.'

'What about coffee?'

'Then I want to take you back to my place and do what I badly wanted to do with you this morning. I can promise you a birthday present you will not forget, *cara*.'

He...*they* had a problem and his solution...? Seduce her right here in a public place! Where anyone could have heard the things he'd said.

It was laughable; he was ridiculous.

Only his voice, the rich, rich bitter chocolate with that curious tactile quality, was not something she found herself able to laugh at. Their glances connected and a faint sigh left her parted lips. Desire zinged along her nerve endings, closing down her logic circuits and opening her pupils wide.

The seconds ticked away and with each one the sexual tension that crackled in the air mounted and the clenched core of desire in Eve's belly tightened. Draco just continued to stare at her with the same soul-stripping intensity, the carnal message in his eyes very clear.

She took a deep breath. 'Yes...'

They both got to their feet in unison, Draco almost knocking his chair over in the process.

He flung a handful of notes on the table without even glancing at the denominations, grabbed her hand and growled.

'Let's get out of here.'

He didn't roll away but remained heavy and hot above her. His face was pressed against her neck, his breath warm and moist against her skin. She liked it, everything about it, the skin-to-skin contact, his weight, the musky smell of sex mingled with soap.

They were lying naked on a massive leather chesterfield in Draco's study. They hadn't managed to make it up the stairs; they had barely even made it out of the cab.

The room was littered with the clothes they had ripped off in a mutual frenzy of haste for skin-to-skin contact.

The frenzy had passed but Eve's breath still came in a series of shallow gasps; her ribcage lifted with each gasp, making the breast not compressed by Draco's head quiver. One arm curled over her head and the other in his hair, she lay on her back, staring, eyes half closed, at the ceiling. Her body was gently humming still in the aftermath of a climax that had rocked her body with wave after wave of intense pleasure.

'How did this happen?' she murmured.

'Do you want bullet points or shall I run through it step by step?' She heard the smile in his voice.

'Neither, but happy birthday to me.'

He curved a hand over her breast. 'I'll second that.'

'Draco…?'

'Give me five minutes.'

She laughed. 'I have to go.' She tried to push him off her but he resisted.

'No,' he groaned.

She arched a brow. 'Please, Draco, I have to.'

With a show of reluctance he rolled away.

Eve felt his eyes on her as she got dressed. His dark stare made her feel self-conscious but also empowered. She could be naked in front of him; she could stutter and not want to die… Was that bad…good…dangerous? She gave her head a tiny shake. Eve just knew it felt good. To have a man like Draco act as though he couldn't get enough of you was a pretty ego-enhancing experience.

Midway through fastening her shirt, she stopped and tilted her head to one side in a listening attitude.

'There's someone here.' She could hear the sound of a door closing and voices...female voices?

'No, I told you—' This time Draco heard them too. He closed his eyes then sat up with a sigh.

'I think there's more than one of them,' she confided in a hushed whisper.

He left the chesterfield in one lithe motion. Reaching for his trousers, he angled her a carnal look that made her insides flip and her eyes glow.

'Hold that thought,' he commanded thickly.

'*That* wasn't what I was thinking.'

He dragged his shirt together; some lies were just too obvious to justify a response. 'Stay here—it'll be safer.'

The comment sent her imagination into overdrive. 'Safe from what? Do you know who it is? Should I call the police?'

'It's nice to know you care, but I can handle this.'

Eve wanted to yell she didn't care after him, but suddenly she had an awful feeling it would be a lie.

CHAPTER TEN

BEFORE HE LEFT the room Draco buttoned up his shirt and dragged a hand through his hair.

The three females who were standing at the far end of the hallway didn't immediately see him when he walked through from the library, and it was Josie who first spotted him.

Her expression was a revealing mix of guilt and relief, which cut a long story short for him.

'Hello, kiddo, so let me guess—your mother sprang you from school to do something educational like—?'

'Shopping in the sales,' Josie supplied with a sheepish shrug.

'Good afternoon, Clare. You look gorgeous, as usual.'

'Draco.' She moved forward to offer each cheek in turn to him for a kiss. 'And you look...' She stopped, a speculative look entering her eyes as she looked at him. 'And you look...' responding to the warning flash in his eyes, she glanced at her daughter '...gorgeous too, darling. Something *definitely* agrees with you.'

'Mother,' Draco greeted Veronica.

'Draco, you should not wander around the house in your bare feet. It gives the wrong impression.'

'To who?'

'Standards,' she responded somewhat mysteriously.

'And I suppose you were just passing...?'

'Do I need a reason to visit my own son?' Veronica broke off, frowning, as a loud noise came from the library. 'Is there someone in there, Draco?'

In the library with the shoe she hadn't dropped clutched to her chest, Eve closed her eyes while the moment stretched and thought, Please, *please*, say no. Hearing the mumbled conversation and not being able to make out what was being said had been frustrating so she had been moving towards the open door when she had dropped her shoe.

'Yes.'

She opened her scrunched eyes and clenched her fists. Would it have killed him to lie?

'Eve, *cara*, come out and say hi to Josie.'

Short of hiding behind the curtains, which did not seem such a terrible option to her at that moment, Eve didn't have much choice. She glanced at her flushed face in the mirror.

'She knows Josie?'

Besides Draco's daughter there were two women in the room. The older one had jaw-length dark hair streaked with silver, and as she glanced her way Eve received the impression of energy and simple elegance. She realised she was looking at Josie in forty years' time—*lucky girl*.

The other was a stunning blue-eyed blonde whose impressive curves were displayed in a tight bandage-style red dress that nipped in her minuscule waist and displayed a cleavage that would have made her a perfect model for Eve's Temptation.

Yes, *stunning* about described her, Eve decided. Her face, figure, her long river-straight blonde hair, everything more than deserved that accolade—stunning.

'Eve!' With the energy of youth but none of the awkwardness, Josie was across the room in moments, her admiring stare on Eve's hair, which fell in a rippling curtain of pre-Raphaelite waves down her narrow back. 'Wow, I just love your hair that way.'

Eve lifted a self-conscious hand to her hair. 'It has a life of its own.'

'Mother, this is Eve Curtis.' Draco took her by the arm and drew her forward. 'Eve, my mother, Veronica Morelli.'

'Mrs Morelli...'

'And this is Clare.' Eve felt his arm go around her shoulder and stiffened.

'I'm his ex-wife,' the blonde said, gliding forward on her five-inch heels and displaying a wide friendly smile. 'It's really nice to meet you, Eve. So where have you been hiding her, Draco? And how long have you two been together?'

'We met yesterday morning,' Draco said evasively.

'All right, I know it's none of my business,' Clare replied.

'I need to get back to the office,' Eve said abruptly.

'Office?' Veronica enquired.

'Eve runs her own company, Mother.'

'Really?' We must have coffee sometime and you can tell me all about your business.' It was obvious from her sudden change of attitude that his mother was now viewing her as potential bride material.

She was embarrassed but Draco had to be hating it. He could have simply outed her there and then as a casual fling but he hadn't, and she even felt a little guilty as she would not have expected this sort of consideration for her feelings from him.

'I guess if you're your own boss you can spend the afternoon…?'

At another warning look from her ex-husband, the blonde subsided.

'Sorry, but I must go—' Eve started.

'And Josie needs to get back to school.'

Josie pouted at her grandmother's pronouncement. 'But Clare said that I could have the day off—we were going shopping and getting our nails done.'

'I'm sure your mother realises that your schooling comes first—and you call your mother Clare now?' This disapproving addition from Veronica drew a wry look from her son.

'Would you mind dropping Josie off at school on your way back to your office, Eve?'

Startled by the request, she nodded. 'Fine.'

The older woman grabbed Josie's hand. 'Come along, Josephina. You need to get into your uniform. We must not keep Miss Curtis waiting.'

'Sorry about the interruption, you two.' Clare smiled as her daughter left the room with her grandmother. 'Sex in the afternoon is just so beautifully decadent and naughty, I always think.'

'You're embarrassing Eve,' Draco chided.

'Really!' Her astonishment seemed genuine. 'Sorry, Draco, it's just when you strolled in here looking all...' She gave a reminiscent little sigh. 'I remember that look.'

Eve felt a sharp stab of something too near jealousy for comfort. She closed her eyes and thought, I have to get out of here. She'd heard of amicable divorces but this was ridiculous!

Veronica Morelli reappeared with a neatly uniformed Josie at her side. 'She couldn't find anything and I'm not surprised. Why you insist on living in this cramped doll's house I will never understand.'

Eve's jaw dropped. If Draco's mother thought this was cramped what was she used to? It must be a castle at least.

'Very nice to meet you both,' Eve lied as she left.

* * *

In the taxi Josie was talkative. 'You have no idea how glad I am that you're with Dad.'

'I'm not—' Eve encountered the teenager's questioning look and closed her mouth. You couldn't tell your lover's teenage daughter that you were just having casual sex with her father, rather than a meaningful relationship.

As she recalled Draco's comment about his daughter trying to find him a wife a worried frown pleated her brow. She didn't want to encourage the girl's fantasy but brutal honesty was obviously not an option. 'I'm glad you're glad.'

'And you're nothing like Dad's usual type...'

Tell me something I didn't already know, Eve thought, an image of his incredibly gorgeous ex-wife drifting into her mind. There had to have been a lot of Clare clones since, and then me.

'I'm not supposed to know he has a type, which is kind of unrealistic but because he never brings them home he thinks I don't know.'

That got Eve's attention. 'He *never* brings them home?' She told herself firmly that she was not going to read anything significant into that.

'You think he does when I'm not there, like

Lily's dad?' Josie shook her head vigorously. 'Lily said she could always tell when her dad's girl-friend had been in their flat as she could *smell* her and things got left behind and moved—and she was right as they got married last month.'

Did Draco's bed smell of her?

'I'm sure it's very hard when a parent decides to remarry.'

'Gosh, no, I'd love it, and Gran would too. She's always nagging him about it, but she doesn't think anyone's good enough for him and Mu— Clare is really bitchy about the ones he dates sometimes. But you're different and if you did marry Dad or even if you were his girlfriend, they wouldn't be able to send me to live with Mum and her fiancé, cos you'd definitely be a stable female influence in my life, wouldn't you?'

Eve digested the stream of artless confidences in silence, finally asking casually, 'Is there a chance of you going to live with your mum?'

Josie shook her head. 'No, Dad promised he won't let it happen, no matter what.'

She sat in the cab until Josie had gone through the school gates, then gave the address of her office to the driver. The cringingly embarrassing scene she had endured had been playing in her head on a loop like background noise since they had left the house, only this time, in the light of Josie's revelations, it took on a very different slant.

They said knowledge was power but Eve didn't feel powerful; she felt grubby and used. The worst part was she had really thought Draco had been sparing her embarrassment, that he had allowed the assumption they were in a relationship to stand uncorrected out of consideration for her feelings.

And I stood there like a puppet feeling...grateful. She felt her temper rise and didn't fight it.

An expression of grim determination spread across her face as she suddenly leaned forward in the cab. 'Change of plan.'

By the time the cab drew up outside Draco's home, in her head Eve had verbally demolished him and made a dignified exit. She was still riding the crest of a wave of righteous anger when she battered on the door with her fist, glaring at one of the several strategically placed cameras above her head that zoomed her way as she did so.

When the door was finally opened Eve, who had been leaning up against it, almost fell inside, narrowly avoiding a collision with the smartly dressed middle-aged woman who had opened it.

'Can I help you?'

Of course he didn't open his own door, she fumed. He probably saved himself for the fun stuff in his life like manipulating and lying.

Eve didn't waste time on small talk. 'I want to see Draco.'

There was a short silence. 'I'm afraid you have the wrong address.'

The outright lie made Eve blink, but she refused to be put off. 'I know he lives here.'

'Now, here is a nice surprise.'

The drawled comment made both women turn their heads as Draco, wearing sweats and a vest, emerged through a door. He had a towel slung around his neck and his skin glistened with a layer of sweat.

Eve reacted to the testosterone-fuelled sight and, forgetting every word of the cutting and incisive speech she'd prepared, she stabbed an accusing finger in his direction and barked, *'You...!'*

Wow, said the voice in her head. *Powerful stuff, Eve, that's really telling him.*

After holding her eyes for a long simmering moment, he turned to the older woman. He unhooked the towel and dragged a hand through his damp hair.

'Thanks, Judith.' The smile was for the older woman but his eyes only left Eve's face for a split second. 'I'll take it from here. You get off and go straight home after your appointment.'

'Are you sure?' The older woman cast a doubtful glance Eve's way as she stepped towards the open door.

'What time is your dental appointment?'

The reminder drew a click of her tongue followed by a wince. 'Gracious, is that the time? You're sure…?'

Eve endured the other woman's suspicious glance, able to be more philosophical about being cast as a dangerous lunatic than she was about her visceral reaction to the raw power of Draco's sweaty body post workout.

Eve waited until the door closed. 'That woman said you didn't live here.'

'She's very protective. She popped in to see if I was all right on her way to the dentist.'

'Do you expect all your staff to lie for you?' All the self-discipline in the world couldn't stop her eyes drifting over his powerful muscular frame. She swallowed and licked her lips, managing to inject the scorn that had been absent from her lustful stare into her voice as she sneered sarcastically, 'You being so weak and defenceless.'

An army of housekeepers couldn't have defended him from the lust that had slammed like a hammer through his body at the sight of her standing there looking mad and so desirable it physically hurt.

Hurt…! Talk about self-delusion!

It seemed amusing to him now that midway through his workout he'd actually convinced himself that he was totally in control and he could go back to feeling smugly superior to men who allowed their hormones to rule their actions.

'I was heading for the shower.' And possibly therapy! It was one thing to recognise all the warning signs of a dangerous addiction, but it was another not to feel the need to fight it.

Why fight something that was so pleasurable? he mused.

Enjoy it while it lasted seemed a much more pragmatic approach to something that was so hot it would inevitably burn itself out soon enough, he told himself.

'If that was an invitation to join you, I'll pass.' She choked, her cheeks heated from the vividly arousing images of water sliding off his slick muscled body.

Ashamed of the heaviness and ache low in her pelvis, Eve dragged her gaze free of the invitation in his heavy-lidded eyes and pretended to look around.

'Your guests gone?'

His glance was drawn to the tears glazing her eyes. 'Are you all right?'

The fake concern after what he'd done brought her teeth together in a silent snarl of disbelief.

'No, I'm not bloody all right. I'm furious.' With him for being a manipulative liar, but mostly Eve's anger was aimed at herself. 'How d-dare you use me? I swore I'd never let any man use me the way my father used mum. You planned it all, didn't you?' she flung wildly. 'It was all cold-blooded calculation.'

The last comment drew a laugh from him. 'Nothing between us is cold-blooded, *cara*. Who is your father?'

Her face froze. 'A bastard like you.'

She saw the flash of anger in his dark eyes and lifted her chin, welcoming the thought of confrontation...then watched incredulously as he began to stroll across the hallway to the central staircase.

'You're walking away?'

'I'm taking a shower before my muscles seize up and we both say things we might regret later.' He had been headed for the shower in the well-equipped basement leisure suite when he had seen her image on one of the security cameras.

'I don't regret anything!'

She'd yelled at him in a way he did not tolerate from anyone else; she'd flung accusations, called him a bastard to his face and created the sort of emotional scene he hated and yet he found he could reply with perfect honesty.

'Neither do I. Feel free to join me,' Draco murmured as he heard her heels clacking behind him on the marble floor.

Eve was panting with the exertion of chasing after him, but only a second behind as she followed him through the door of his bedroom suite. It wasn't until the door swung shut with a click that sounded awfully final behind her that she questioned the wisdom of her actions. A second later she was definitely panicking.

'What do you think you're doing?' A shrill note crept into her voice as she watched him peel the vest over his head. His back was to her and as he stretched his arms her eyes were riveted to the play of muscle under his olive-toned skin; each ripple and contraction made her stomach flip and quiver. He was perfect anatomically and aesthetically.

He turned to her with an expression of innocent surprise on his too handsome face and as his hands dropped to his sides, his feet slightly apart, his attitude was one of blatantly sexual arrogant challenge and there was nothing contrived about it—this was him.

Her breath snagged in her throat as, still holding her eyes, he dropped the vest he had peeled off onto a chair. 'I told you, I'm taking a shower.' His eyes glittered with sardonic humour but he managed to sound mildly surprised by the question.

'I want to talk to you.' She struggled to maintain an air of subtle disdain while under the cold surface her hormones had gone into dramatic free fall. Whatever else he was, Draco was the most beautiful thing she had ever seen with more raw sex appeal in his little finger than most men had in their entire bodies.

'Nothing stopping you, *cara.*' He bent to unlace his trainers, even this casual action made riveting by the casual animal grace that characterised all his actions. He kicked off one shoe and then the other.

Watching him through the utterly inadequate shield of her lashes, Eve felt as though she were going to explode. What, she speculated, lifting a hand to her head, would the autopsy report as the cause of death…fury or lust?

Both would be accurate as this man somehow managed to tap directly into her most primal urges. He was the incarnation of everything that she had sworn to herself she would reject.

'So if you change your mind about joining me…
the offer's still open.' Holding her eyes, he smiled
and reached for the cord tie on his sweat pants.

Her eyes dropped and she felt the blush begin.
Turning on her heel and presenting her rigid back
to him, she missed his smile of satisfaction.

CHAPTER ELEVEN

'A TEMPTING OFFER, but I'll pass.'

Unwilling to admit even to herself, *especially* to herself, how true this was, how much she was tempted to join him in the shower, Eve picked up a cushion from the pile thrown artistically on a chaise longue set against the far wall and began banging it. When it was battered out of shape she moved on to another, plumping it so enthusiastically that his response was barely audible above the thwacking.

'Suit yourself.'

She waited a few moments then risked looking over her shoulder. The discarded pants lay in a crumpled heap on the floor and with a deep sigh she let herself fall back on the cushions. She concentrated on steady breathing in and out, but the tension that tied her muscles in knots stubbornly persisted.

This was not going as she had anticipated.

Midway through telling herself she'd have to up her game, she heard the shower start up in the adjoining bathroom. A glazed expression slid into her eyes before she let them close, but that made it worse. Images crowded into her head of a steam-filled room, water sliding off slick brown skin, droplets gleaming on the sprinkling of chest hair that became a thin directional arrow down his flat belly.

The memory of the open invitation he had issued echoed in her head, feeding the ache of need that throbbed through her. She lifted a despairing hand to her head where increasingly vivid carnal images were playing on a loop and wondered how it was possible to be so furious with someone, know perfectly well they were using you, and yet still want them so badly… Her eyes opened and her hand fell limply away.

Was she finally becoming the person she had never forgiven her mother for being? The thought worked better than a cold shower and coincided with a sudden silence as the water in the bathroom went off and a switch in her head went back on.

She went pale at the thought of how close she'd come to running towards temptation and opening that door. Where Draco was concerned she appeared to have no shame or self-respect. Genes will out, she warned herself, and, shaking her head, she surged to her feet. Recognising a weakness in yourself meant you could do something about it—there was always a choice.

Her mother had had a choice and she'd made the wrong one—twice. Eve had no intention of repeating Sarah's mistakes.

She weighed her options, and it didn't take long to make her decision. She'd pass on the satisfaction of having the last word and put a safe distance between herself and Draco.

Run away. She released a slow measured breath. It was a plan—definitely a plan.

But before Eve could put this plan into action or even place one foot in front of the other Draco, whistling softly under his breath, strolled into the room barefoot and her urgent need to escape immediately became less urgent—a lot less urgent.

His dark hair had been slicked back messily with his hands and was still dripping water, leaving dark patches on the white shirt he wore.

Emotions raw and her senses heightened to a painful degree, Eve knew with total certainty that

that image, this vignette, had imprinted itself indelibly in her memory. For as long as she lived she would remember the way he looked and the way she felt.

'Did you miss me?' he asked, tucking the dangling tails of his shirt into the waist of dark trousers as he watched the expressions flicker across her face. When her mask was down she had the most expressive features he had ever encountered.

She tipped her chin. Sometimes the truth, however unpalatable, was the best defence. 'With every fibre of my being.'

The sexy husk in her voice sent a visceral shudder through his body, and his nerve endings tingled the way they had when her hair had brushed his bare skin.

'Right, now I'm all yours.' His grin flashed as he held his arms wide in invitation and drawled, 'Double entendre totally intended, in case you were wondering.'

'I wasn't.' Suddenly Eve was fed up with the games and the smart talk. She was glad now she hadn't made good her getaway; she would have always regretted not telling him what she thought of him.

Holding his eyes, she planted her hands on her hips, unwittingly drawing his attention to the gentle curves, and looked him up and down. See how you like it, she thought.

Problem was, he did seem to like it! There was a glimmer of admiration in his slow appreciative smile as he purred, 'Like what you're seeing, *cara*?'

She flushed and thought, Who wouldn't? Draco was the epitome of virile alpha-male perfection.

'You used me.' She swallowed, recognising that it was irrational that the knowledge hurt. After all, there was no trust between them, no bond that had been betrayed—just her own stupidity.

The quiet accusation caused his smile to fade. Jaw clenched, his dark brows drawn into a heavy line above his eyes, he sketched a frown that deepened as, unable to resist the compulsion, he let his glance drift over her body, seeing the smooth sleek lines and soft curves beneath the clothes, remembering the silky softness of her delicious skin that made his core temperature climb.

The powerful kick of his libido scored the angles of his carved cheeks with dark colour. The cold shower he had just endured had provided a temporary relief from the insatiable hunger, but now it was back and he could barely think past the desire to sink into her, feel her close tight as a silken glove around him.

'I think there was some mutual using,' he husked. 'And the way I recall it you had no complaints.'

She narrowed her eyes, folded her arms across her chest in an unconsciously self-protective gesture and angled a look of simmering contempt up at his lean, handsome face.

'You know exactly what I'm talking about!' she charged furiously.

Know?

He almost laughed. He knew nothing except that this had never happened to him before. It wasn't just his body; this woman had taken up residence in his head. He shrugged, refusing to acknowledge the surge of panic that slid through him. This thing between them would run its course, burn bright, and then become a delicious memory.

'How about you spell it out just to be on the safe side?' he suggested.

'Spell...let me see.' Finger on her chin, she pretended to think about it. 'B A S T A R D, exclamation mark. You are afraid of losing custody of Josie so I'm a token girlfriend…a female influence, a—' she sketched quotation marks in the air and drawled with disgust '—"stable relationship" to waft under the nose of your ex… No wonder you wanted me out of there before I could tell them the truth.'

'And what truth is that?'

'I'm just another of your one-night stands.'

'Bitterness…yet I seem to recall you wouldn't have it any other way, *cara*. Or are you moving the goalposts now?'

'I'm not bitter, I'm mad!'

'If you say so…and to be accurate it was not just at night—we already did night and day.'

Feeling an errant nerve jump in her soft jaw, Eve looked away.

'And you look about as stable as a diva having a meltdown,' he teased.

But, hell, it suited her! Eve had been repressing her passionate nature so long she probably believed that she was the tight-lipped, buttoned-up robot she liked people to think she was—it was a role she preferred to hide behind. To know that he was the only man who had seen behind the façade made him feel... He frowned, struggling to condense and compress all the emotions this woman shook loose in him into just one word... one sentence...one book!

'If I'd known you wanted to make friends with my mother and ex-wife I'd have taken Josie to school myself, though for future reference, just in case your paths cross again, I feel you should know that intelligence agencies all over the world have adopted my mother's interrogation techniques. And how was I meant to introduce you, by the way? This is Eve—we're just having sex?'

'So you were being kind.'

'There was a certain amount of self-interest involved,' he admitted.

'You used me,' she insisted, clinging tightly to her righteous indignation even though what had seemed like a legitimate accusation on the taxi drive back now sounded a little bit hysterical. 'You set it all up, got me here knowing that your ex would—'

'Would what exactly? You seriously believe I arranged to have my ex-wife, my mother and my teenage daughter walk in on me naked with a woman in the middle of the afternoon?'

She had, but when he put it like that… The sliver of doubt in Eve's head widened as, unable to admit she was totally in the wrong, she conceded, 'I don't suppose you expected your mother to be there too.'

'Thank you for that.'

His sarcasm made her teeth ache.

'For the record, I never expect my mother. She believes strongly in the advantage of surprise. Since my father died she is bored and I have become her project. Or, more correctly, getting me married to someone suitable has become her project.'

'So you admit it. You let her think that we are… are…are… Will you stop looking at me as though I'm a bug under a microscope or something?'

'In a relationship?' he finished her earlier sentence.

'We're not in a relationship, we're having sex!' she bellowed before adding through gritted teeth. '*Were* having sex.'

Eve would have preferred her over-the-top reaction to make him angry, not curious, as she struggled to retain her defiance in the face of his searching scrutiny.

'Why is the distinction so important to you?'

Wanting to aggravate him, she deliberately misunderstood. 'I like good grammar.'

'Not that distinction, the one between having sex and being in a relationship. Is this to do with your mother and Latimer...?' he pressed shrewdly.

Feeling the pressure of his stare and reacting defensively, she stuck out her chin. 'This isn't about me, it's about you; and anyway, I don't think you're anyone to lecture me about relationships. According to your daughter you change women the way most men change their socks.'

Draco recognised classic deflection when he heard it; he used it himself on occasion. But unlike Eve he did so consciously. He might not be guilty of contriving the situation earlier as she'd accused, but he had felt no compunction about taking advantage of it. For the first time in months, his mother had left without dropping heavy hints about moving in to take care of Josie.

'You didn't have to pump my daughter for information, Eve. You could have just asked me if you'd wanted to know anything about me.'

Eve rolled her eyes in response, while Draco

made a discovery that utterly shocked him. He had meant what he'd said.

He had become adept at recognising the warning signs when a woman wanted more than he was prepared to give, and even the suggestion that they were looking for weaknesses in his emotional barriers was usually a signal to walk away—but now he was inviting Eve in to walk around his head!

'I didn't pump!' she exploded, her eyes flashing green fire at the charge. 'You're Josie's favourite subject.'

He arched an ebony brow. 'Not yours?'

'Oh, I find you fascinating,' she trilled, taking pleasure from the flicker of something that might have been unease she saw move at the backs of his eyes.

'So you have been discussing me with my daughter.'

'You know how it is when girls are together...'

He responded to this with a veiled look that made it impossible for her to read his reaction— was he worried...? She hoped so!

'Don't play games with me, Eve.' For the first time his low voice held a thread of anger as he took a step towards her.

'Am I meant to be scared?' The adrenaline rush that sharpened all her senses to a painful degree made her respond in an uncharacteristically reckless fashion—though compared with the reckless steps she'd taken recently this one was fairly innocuous.

He reached out and took her chin in his fingers, tilting her face up to him. 'Some people are.' Power, which for Draco was a by-product of his financial success, not an aim in itself, meant he was used to seeing the fear and envy that was often behind people's smiles. They saw the public image and not the man and he had no problem with that; he had no wish to be understood or universally loved. 'Not you,' he said positively.

There was no escape from his searching stare—the truth was Draco himself didn't frighten her. It was the way he made her feel that was beginning to scare Eve witless…

Still resisting the possibility she had more in common with her mother than she was prepared to or could admit, Eve shook her head and countered, 'Should I be?'

His hand fell from her face to her shoulder, where his thumb moved restlessly back and forth over her collarbone as he stared down into her face feeling a sudden surge of protectiveness.

'Probably. I don't want to hurt you.' But that didn't mean she wouldn't be collateral damage in what passed for his love life. He felt a sudden knife thrust of anger at himself. She was not meant to be so vulnerable but she was—and he'd seen it right from the beginning.

She watched him warily. His honesty had finally drained all the anger from her; maybe he deserved some in return.

'I thought you had planned it all,' she admitted in a small voice.

Even though his hand fell away he remained so close that she imagined she could feel the warmth of his body.

'After Josie told me about the custody battle and that your ex is using the emotional vacuum of what passes for your love life as leverage...' Her eyes lifted. 'No insult intended.'

The tension in his jaw relaxed as he read the sincerity in her face.

'I decided that when you came to my office this morning you knew exactly what was going to happen...I mean...'

'That we'd end up having wild sex in my study and my family would walk in on us.'

On the receiving end of his dark intense stare, she felt her temperature shoot up several degrees. 'I'm trying to apologise.'

His eyebrows rose incredulously.

'I can now see that it was—'

'Spontaneous?'

She frowned fiercely at the interruption. 'A series of coincidences.' He saw a flicker of guilt move like a shadow across her face. A soft heart could be a major disadvantage in the business world, and it made him wonder how she had got so far.

'Apology accepted. You had the details about Clare's custody claim from Josie… Is Josie worried about it?'

He'd thought his daughter could tell him anything…but for the first time Draco stopped to consider the suddenly shockingly real possibility that his daughter really was losing out not having a stepmother she could bond with. He didn't like the thought of Josie opening up to someone who was almost a total stranger, *needing* to open up to another woman as she had done with Eve.

His little girl was growing up and did the awful, boring Edward have a point? Was she lacking a female role model?

'Josie has total faith in your ability to sort it.' And just about anything else that might crop up. When the teenager spoke of her father, even when she was complaining, it was obvious that she adored him and had complete trust in his ability to keep her safe.

The way her own mother had kept her safe… Had Eve always appreciated it?

Draco nodded, feeling a surge of relief, his concern allayed slightly, yet the doubts that had been awoken remained there just below the surface.

'Are you really not worried about the custody claim? I mean, don't courts normally favour mothers?'

'Potential custody claim.'

The smooth correction drew a frown from Eve. 'You don't think she'll go through with it?'

Was he really as confident as he sounded? Or was this an example of his feelings for his ex-wife clouding his judgement?

In his place, with a great kid like Josie to protect… But she wasn't in his place, Eve reminded herself, and Josie wasn't her child. Which meant she could be totally objective, unlike Draco, and probably any other male when it came to a woman like Clare.

'Josie has never lived with her mother?'

'No, never.' He arched a brow. 'Do you think that's wrong?'

A few minutes had been long enough for Eve to see that the beautiful woman was the last person in the world that should be given charge of any child, let alone one as special as Josie who, in her opinion, deserved a lot better.

'I think that depends on the mother and the circumstances,' she said tactfully.

'Clare walked out when Josie was a baby.'

'How could she have done that?' In Eve's mind a woman was hard-wired to care for her baby before anything else, and there were women who gave their lives for their babies.

She supposed women like Clare were the flip side of the coin. Yet she still couldn't see how any woman could walk out and abandon her baby and she never would.

'Was there…someone else or was it post-natal depression, perhaps?' she suggested tentatively.

'No, she just got bored.'

Watching her face, he sank down onto a sofa. 'Take the weight off,' he said, patting the arm in invitation.

'I'll pass.'

He grinned and Eve almost responded, making up for the near slip with a really fierce frown. She needed her anger to hide behind... Her eyes widened in alarm before she lowered her eyelashes protectively to mask her expression... Where did that thought come from?

'Clare loses interest in things very quickly.'

Shocked by the suggestion, Eve looked up. 'Even in her own daughter?'

He ran a hand down his jaw. 'In anything.' A fact that Edward had yet to learn.

Eyes on her face, he didn't miss another flicker of repugnance as he let his broad shoulders relax into the buttoned leather back of the chesterfield, giving a grunt as he stretched his long legs out and crossed one ankle over the other.

His fitness regime was pretty brutal but the previous night followed by today's session with Eve had left him with some muscles he hadn't known he had aching. Eve in his bed beat a treadmill any day!

'So you no longer think this afternoon was part of some dastardly plan of mine.'

She shifted uncomfortably and shrugged. 'Maybe not,' she admitted.

His brows lifted. 'Maybe?'

Maybe she deserved to squirm a little…? 'All right, *definitely not*—'

'This custody thing.'

'That's worrying you now, isn't it?'

The question in Eve's mind was, why hadn't it been worrying him all along?

'Look, this isn't Clare, it's her fiancé who is driving this campaign for custody of Josie, and he has his own political agenda. What he doesn't realise is that Clare is *allowing* him to manipulate her. Don't let the ditsy blonde stuff fool you; Clare is smart and when she needs to be, she's totally ruthless.'

This chilling assessment made Eve shiver, all the more so because it came from Draco. He clearly still had feelings for the mother of his child—nothing else in Eve's opinion made sense of the fact he seemed to tolerate and make excuses for

Clare doing just about anything. The question was how deep were those feelings?

'And you're all right with that?'

'She loves Josie.'

But do you love Clare…? Eve just stopped herself voicing the question that loomed large in her head. What would be the point when she already knew the answer? No man could make so many allowances for a woman who had left him literally holding the baby unless he had real feelings for her. Maybe he couldn't admit it, but it was obvious to her that the only reason that Draco had not been in a real relationship since his divorce was that he was still hooked on his beautiful, selfish ex-wife and the mother of his child.

Eve was glad she was not competing with that!

'No, I'm not in love with Clare.'

Her eyes flew wide. 'I w-wasn't thinking that!'

His brows lifted in a sceptical arc.

'Look, I know you don't want to know what I think.'

Draco arched a sable brow. 'But you're going to tell me anyway…?'

'Maybe you shouldn't be too complacent about this custody issue; courts can be unpredictable.'

He looked thoughtful. 'You think I'm compla-cent?'

She thought he was gorgeous. 'There's no harm taking precautions.'

He nodded slowly.

'Look, if you want them to carry on thinking that we are…together in the short term, obviously while we are still…'

'Having sex?'

'If we *are* still having sex?'

'For Josie's sake?'

He was not making this easy. 'For *my* sake,' she admitted. 'Then that's fine. If, of course, you *are* up for it.'

'Come here and I'll show you how up for it I am.'

It took very little persuasion to make her fall into his lap.

CHAPTER TWELVE

EVE WAS APPLYING a final sweep of mascara when Hannah swept into the room. She spun her stool around to face her friend, who was already in full regal evening dress, the empire line not quite disguising her pregnancy bump.

'How is Kamel?'

'Oh, fine, according to him.' Hannah's eye roll could not disguise her concern for her husband's health. 'But in the real world he has a temperature of a hundred and two and looks like death warmed up in a gorgeous way... He's impossible! Why can't he do man flu like every other man instead of...? God, but I wish I could stay with him.' Her friend took a deep breath, pasted on a bright smile and muttered, 'But duty calls and the doctors swear that the antibiotics should have kicked in by the morning. He's very lucky it's not pneumonia...and if he'd left it any longer...'

'He'll be fine.'

'Of course he will…you have no idea, Eve, how grateful I am that you're here. This is the first time I've ever done one of these things on my own and Kamel is the charity patron, so it matters just having a friendly face in the room. I hope I'll—'

'You'll do amazingly, and I know you're grateful because you've told me about ten billion times, which was unnecessary, as was the makeover. Or maybe it wasn't,' she admitted, glancing down at the designer gown she had selected from the rail of similar garments her friend had wheeled into the room.

'You look stunning, Evie.'

Eve looked up, a faint flush on her cheeks. A few weeks ago she wouldn't have believed Hannah, nor for that matter would she have had the confidence required to wear the dramatic full-length red dress that clung to her body like a second skin, hugging her breasts, emphasising her tiny waist and softly curved hips before flaring at the knee flamenco style.

Being with Draco over the past weeks had done that, had given her that confidence in her own sexuality and sensual allure. That was the plus, that and great sex, and his earthy laugh… The downside… She pinned a smile on her face and promised herself she wouldn't go there tonight.

Who was she kidding? She carried it with her like another layer of skin. She had fallen in love with Draco and she had to hide it, disguise it, bury it. There was simply no other way of dealing with this situation.

She had fallen, deeply, for a man who was everything she had spent her adult life avoiding, and they weren't even in a real relationship. But the important thing was, it was on her terms.

She squeezed her eyes closed as she experienced a moment of scalding self-disgust. At least Mum had been honest. On her terms, indeed…!

In reality this meant she wasn't available when Draco clicked his fingers, even if she was. Even if this meant she spent some really miserable nights when she could have been sharing his bed lying alone. She repeatedly told herself it was worth it, because it meant that she was in control.

She recognised the self-delusion but she wasn't brave enough to admit it.

'And I can't remember the last time I saw you with your hair loose. I hardly recognised you,' continued Hannah.

'I hardly recognise myself these days,' Eve admitted quietly as the two women left the room.

With cameras recording every inflection and under the glitter of chandeliers Hannah gave the speech on her husband's behalf with charm and dignity. In fact, she was so good that for about ten seconds Eve even stopped wondering about Draco.

What was he doing?

Who was he talking to?

What would he have thought of her in this dress?

Draco was putting in a token appearance towards the end of the evening because Kamel was a good friend and he had always despised men who forgot their friends the moment they became romantically involved—and he wasn't. Eve and he had a civilised relationship; while it was different from his other liaisons in many ways, it was still not permanent.

Josie having recently opted for the weekly boarding option at school was the only reason Eve slept over at his place, though not quite as often as he would have liked. Eve had a life he wasn't part of; he had a life she wasn't part of...

He was just telling himself how well this situation worked for him when these worlds meshed.

It was totally unexpected. He simply turned his head to see what the titled blond-haired guy he had been introduced to when he arrived was staring at, and it turned out to be a who. *His* Eve, looking totally at ease, smiling, charming, in a red dress that was slinky and sexy and… He felt his core temperature jump as his eyes followed the sinuous curves of her body. This was not an outfit she should be wearing outside the confines of their bedroom!

Not even conscious that he had blanked an ambassador who had been approaching him with his hand outstretched, Draco strode across the room.

'What the hell are you doing here?' he thundered in Eve's ear.

It was Hannah, standing beside her friend, who blinked as her gaze moved from Eve to the tall figure who stood there glowering like some dark avenging angel.

Eve's shock gave way to indignation. 'Is there any reason I shouldn't be here?' she retorted with deceptive calm.

'You might have mentioned it to me.'

Her feathery brows lifted. 'You're here; did you mention it to me?' She lifted a hand to cover her mouth and said softly from behind it, 'There's a film crew here tonight, Draco. Do you really want to broadcast this to the world?' Removing her hand and raising her voice, she added brightly, 'You know Hannah, of course.'

Draco tipped his head, his eyes not leaving Eve as he said, 'Princess. I am sorry to hear Kamel is unwell.' Then to Eve, he added, 'I'm going home. Are you coming?'

Hannah's gasp was audible.

Draco flashed a look her way then back to his lover. 'You didn't even tell your best friend we are together?' He thought women shared every-thing...everything that mattered anyway. It felt like a betrayal. Was she ashamed of him or didn't he even rate gossip?

Eve narrowed her eyes. 'No, I'm not coming.'

He gave a magnificent shrug. 'Fine. I'm leav-ing for New York on Friday.'

'Have a good flight.'

'You will be back for my birthday?' Josie asked over the phone.

In his hotel room Draco left the window and

the view of Central Park. 'Aren't I always there for your birthday?'

'Just checking. It should be a good party. Aunt Gabby is cooking all my favourite food.'

'You're being good for your aunt Gabby, I hope.'

'I'm always good and she loves having me. Ask her if you like—she's here.'

'I'll take your word for it. Josie, I was wondering if you've seen—' He stopped suddenly.

'Have I what…? Sorry, Dad, the line's not so good.'

The line was working a hell of a lot better than his brain! He was so desperate for news of Eve, any scrap or small detail, that he'd been about to milk his teenage daughter for information on her.

What the hell was he doing?

He had lost count of the number of times he had picked up the phone, hungry to hear her voice, but he'd never dialled the number. And why? Because he'd been proving a point. They had not spoken since the night of that damned charity ball.

Pathetic!

All he'd actually proved was that he was gutless. What else did you call a man too afraid to admit he needed a woman, needed to hear her voice, see her smile, watch her fall asleep?

His chest lifted in a silent sigh; he was afraid to admit that he'd finally fallen in love. The admission came with a certain sense of relief; love had made a fool of him once and he'd sworn it would never happen again. But it had.

'You still there, Dad?'

Draco stared at the phone in his hand blankly for a moment before lifting it to his ear.

'I'm fine.' He wasn't but he would be, he thought.

'I said do you mind if I ask Eve…to my birthday party…please?'

'That would be fine.'

Eve had been nervous about meeting Mark Tyler, but it wasn't nearly as awkward as she had imagined. By the time they were drinking their coffee they had discovered they had a lot in common and were talking as though they'd known each other all their lives.

If things had been different they might have. As the thought registered in her brain, she looked at the hand he had laid on hers and sighed.

Across the table Mark looked concerned. 'Are

you all right?' He caught the direction of Eve's gaze and, flushing slightly, went to move the protective hand he had instinctively placed over the smaller one that lay on the table, but as he lifted it her wrist turned and her fingers curled around his.

Their eyes met and clung, and her voice was thick with the same emotions that shone in her eyes as Eve shook her head.

'I'm fine; it's just…I…'

'I know,' he acknowledged.

Coffee finished, the bill paid, Mark suggested he walk her back to her flat rather than call a cab. As it was a beautiful clear evening and she wasn't ready for it to end yet, Eve agreed.

Outside the pavement was wet but it had stopped raining and the night sky was bright and clear, or at least as bright and clear as it ever got in the City.

Eve walked straight into a puddle, splashing her new shoes and tights.

'*Singin' in the Rain*,' they both said in unison and then laughed.

'One of my favourite films,' Eve said.

'A classic,' Mark agreed. 'So you're not sorry you came?'

Eve had admitted to him how nearly she hadn't,

how even at the last minute she had almost choked. She still hadn't got over the shock of being contacted by a half-brother who hadn't known she existed until he had been going through his dead father's things and who now wanted to meet her.

'I'm glad we met. I don't know why I always assumed you knew about me…probably because I knew about you, even though I'm not meant to,' she said.

'I was scared stiff,' her half-brother admitted with a laugh.

'You were?'

'Amy encouraged me; she said it was the right thing to do and then when I saw you at the charity thing the other week—well, Amy made me come over.'

Eve smiled. Mark had brought his wife into the conversation constantly; he clearly adored her, which was wonderful for him. The relationship she had always envied him with his…*their* father had been pretty awful, apparently. Lord Charlford had bullied his son and heir, taking every opportunity to belittle him. It was his wife who had given Mark his confidence back and given him the strength to escape his father's toxic influence.

'Tell me to mind my own business, Eve—Amy always says I'm too pushy!—but do you…have anyone in your life? The man I saw you with… Morelli, perhaps?'

They had reached her building and Eve paused and turned around to face her half-brother. 'There is someone,' she admitted. 'But I'm not sure—'

'If he's *the* one?'

'We've only been together a couple of months but…oh, yes, he's the one for me. I'm just not sure…' Eve's voice terminated on a tearful wobble and she was horrified to feel her eyes fill as she gulped past an emotional constriction the size of a boulder in her aching throat '…if I'm the one for him. He's…' She stopped and shook her head, the lamp light picking out the tear that escaped and slid down her cheek.

Since he'd left for New York after that night almost three weeks ago now, she hadn't heard a word from Draco other than a pretty terse text when he had landed. She had told herself she hadn't expected more, but of course in reality she had.

She'd had a lot of time on her hands to think about her expectations regarding Draco and recognise how unrealistic they were. She had finally admitted to herself that she wanted all the things that she had once scorned. She wanted to love a man to distraction and she wanted to be loved the same way, and it very much looked as though she was not going to get either of those things, as Draco couldn't give her what she needed.

Self-respect and simple common sense had told her that this was a crunch point in their relation-ship. When Draco returned she owed it to both of them to be honest with him and if he couldn't give her what she needed it was time to move on. She understood now, if her mother really did love Charles Latimer as she loved Draco, why she had stayed with him. Eve could see herself slipping too easily into the same sort of arrangement, but dying a little more each day as her self-respect was eroded.

The thought filled her with utter horror but so did the prospect of never seeing Draco again and that was what it would involve. There were no half measures.

Mark lifted a hand and blotted the tear with his thumb, smiling down into her tearful face. 'You're unhappy. I'm sorry.' His handsome face tightened with anger as he added softly, 'Whoever he is, he's a fool.'

'Don't be nice...' she sniffed '...or I'll cry. I don't know what's wrong with me just lately.' Only yesterday she had had to leave a meeting because she'd started to cry when someone had shown her a picture of a litter of kittens her friend had rescued after someone had tied them in a sack and thrown them into a rubbish skip.

'Don't worry, I'm used to tears. Since she's been pregnant Amy cries at anything and everything.'

Her mother, Hannah and now this Amy were all pregnant. Sometimes it felt as though she were the only person in the world who wasn't!

She went still, and her legs began to tremble as a coldness crept over her body, invading every cell with a terrible dread as the feelings swirling through her coalesced into one question!

'Oh, God!'

'What is it?' Mark watched in alarm as the last vestiges of colour left her face.

His concerned voice shook Eve out of her daze. She struggled to act normally, forcing a smile and shaking her head. 'Just a thought, that's all.

Something I should have considered but I didn't…
Silly, really.'

Silly was perhaps not the most appropriate word
to describe a potentially life-changing event, and
the more she thought about it, the more… No,
she thought, closing that door. She would not and
could not think about it now. She needed to know
for sure first and that couldn't happen until tomorrow unless…?

She scrunched her brow, trying to remember if
the supermarket on the corner stayed open twenty-
four seven and, if they did, did they stock preg-
nancy-test kits?

'Look, I'd invite you in for coffee but I'm a bit
tired.'

Mark nodded, kissed her cheek, then hugged
her. Eve planted a reciprocal kiss on his clean-
shaven cheek and hugged him back.

'You will come to Charlford to visit, won't you?
Amy is longing to meet you. The place is upside
down as she's ripping out and tearing down everything that reminds her of Dad—she always
said he made her skin crawl. But after I found out
about you… She says the best way we can punish
him is by having good lives.'

'Amy sounds…I'd love…' Her voice trailed away.

Mark, his hand on her shoulder, turned to follow the direction of her wide-eyed, shocked stare. He turned just in time to see the fist that a moment later connected with his jaw and sent him sprawling.

With a cry Eve was on her knees beside her brother. 'Mark, are you all right?'

Holding his jaw, Mark shook his head. 'Fine. He took me by surprise, that's all.' The glazed expression in his green eyes was replaced by one of anger as he looked up at the tall man who stood over them. It was mixed with a healthy helping of fear as the man was big in a lean, athletic way, a real tough customer.

'What the hell are you doing, Draco?' Eve demanded, fitting a clean tissue to the blood seeping from the corner of her brother's mouth as she sat back on her heels to glare up at him.

The red haze that had descended when Draco had seen the guy touch Eve's cheek and then tenderly embrace her was slowly receding, leaving an anger that was equally lethal but as cold as surgical steel.

'I would ask you the same question but it's very obvious,' he bit out.

'Oh, I am so, *so* sorry, Mark.'

Mark took the tissue from her.

'And he's sorry too, aren't you, Draco…?' Eve said.

'No.'

The unequivocal response drew a glare from Eve, who lifted her head to tell him exactly what she thought of him but he was gone… She turned her head to see him walking away down the street. 'Stay there and don't move,' she said to Mark. Her jaw tightened with determination. 'I have something I need to do.'

Mark caught her arm. 'Leave it, Eve. The guy is dangerous.'

Eve let out a scornful snort. 'I'm not scared of him!' she declared.

He was walking and she was running but it took her fifty yards before she caught up with Draco. As she drew level with him she caught his arm.

She was panting to catch her breath as Draco swung back, his lips curled in a snarl, his eyes as cold as ice chips.

Her eyes searched his lean face. 'Are you mad?'

One corner of his mouth lifted in a sneer. 'Not any more.' For weeks he had fought the knowledge that he loved her, then finally admitted that he was afraid. He'd felt he had moved forward when in reality it turned out he'd been right all along. Loving someone always ended badly.

His cryptic reply just added another layer to all the other layers of confusion in her head—him being here when she knew he was in the States, his attack on Mark, his attitude now as he looked at her as though she were something unpleasant he had stepped in. She was too shocked to be angry or even hurt.

'You're not even here.' Stupid thing to say, Eve, she told herself as her eyes travelled the long, lean length of his broad-shouldered, muscle-packed frame, seeing but still not quite believing he was here. That this was happening.

'Yes, I can see how that might be inconvenient for you,' he drawled.

There was a heavy beat of silence as she waited, fully anticipating that any second now a light would go on in her brain and she'd understand what was happening. But there was no light, just the aftertaste from the acid bite of his sarcasm.

She saw his hands clench into fists, and the tension that was rolling off him in waves had a physical presence.

'What are you doing here?' If she could work that out maybe the rest would fall into place but, no, it wouldn't, because nothing would explain him hitting Mark and nothing, she thought, feeling a stab of anger, would excuse it.

His jaw clenched as he realised he'd nearly made the mistake of his life. 'Spoiling your evening. I suppose you do know he's married.'

Her green eyes still shocked and glazed like someone who had just been jolted out of a trance, she blinked. She followed the direction of the sharp, contemptuous movement of Draco's head to where her half-brother had got to his feet and was walking towards them.

'Mark? Yes, I know.'

Forehead furrowed, she tried to figure this out. What was the relevance of Mark's marriage? Did he know her half-brother? Was there some sort of feud between them, though she had not imagined until now that Draco was the sort of man who resolved feuds with his fists. Up to this point she had only seen Draco be controlled and cool, the last man in the world she had imagined losing control. Not that he didn't have a passionate nature, but outside the bedroom he kept those passions on a tight leash.

She was relieved to see that her half-brother seemed all right, no thanks to Draco. Worried for his safety if he followed after her, she waved her hand and yelled, 'No, Mark, it's fine.' The last thing she wanted was to be in the middle of a brawl.

Had Draco thought she was in danger? The idea might have worked if he hadn't walked away immediately afterwards, and if it hadn't been for that look he'd given her, the coruscating contempt in his eyes in that last dismissive glare…

Turning back to Draco, she said in a fierce voice, 'You lay a finger on him, you bully, and I'll…just don't…' She expelled a shaky sigh. 'You hit him, you really hit him!' That part still didn't seem real; none of this seemed real.

She knew the man was married and she had been totally brazen about it. Draco searched Eve's face for some sign, some little spark of guilt, and saw none…nothing. How could he have got it so wrong?

Mark reached them, the bruises already coming out on one side of his face, the sight of which made Eve feel sick. She moved to stand between the two men. 'Leave him alone,' she warned again.

Draco's jaw clenched at her protective gesture. 'I'm curious…is it the title?'

Eve blinked. 'What are you talking about?'

'Is that the attraction?' He slid a look of smouldering contempt Mark's way and she felt her brother take an involuntary step back. Eve for one didn't blame him. Draco was being positively intimidating! 'Or do pretty blond boys do it for you now?'

'Pretty?' What on earth…? Mark, he meant Mark, who was not pretty, but definitely handsome, in a much less aggressively masculine way than Draco. When illumination came it was dazzling, and with total clarity she finally realised what Draco had seen—or rather what he thought he had seen.

Draco thought that he had caught her in an assignation with a lover!

Ignoring Mark's restraining hand, she stepped forward, her hand extended towards Draco.

'Or does your deceitful little soul enjoy the illicit thrill of sneaking around?' Draco accused.

Her hand fell away.

The shocked hurt in her eyes made him pause, anger, guilt and jealousy twisting inside him, but only briefly. Had she considered his feelings when she got into bed with his pretty lordship? She had zero loyalty and did she ever consider anyone's feelings but her own? He'd seen qualities in her that weren't there, the same way he'd felt a deeper bond where there wasn't one. There was just sex, as she'd always insisted.

'Or is it just a case of like mother, like daughter? Where is your father in all of this?'

Eve was not even conscious she had raised her hand until the whiplash crack made her jump back in shock. Only she hadn't jumped; Mark had pulled her back after she'd slapped Draco across the face.

Mark held her back with a protective arm, anger making him feel brave as he faced Draco. 'He's dead. Her father is dead; *our* father is dead.'

Draco froze, the blood draining from his face as his gaze moved between the two faces staring back at him with similar expressions of disgust and loathing.

'He's your brother? Charlford was your father?' he said in a strangled voice. He was struggling to take in the information as panic slid through his body, freezing his brain. He had messed up big time! 'I thought…'

'You thought that I was cheating on you and you also implied that my mother has questionable morals,' Eve said coldly.

'I didn't say that!'

Even as he protested he realised that it didn't matter what he said; there was no going back. She would never forgive him—he had insulted her mother, and he'd punched a man…her brother!

She was looking at him with loathing in her beautiful eyes and he deserved it.

The shame of having lost the control he prided himself on, the shame of acting like some sort of Neanderthal was a bitter taste in his mouth, and the words he wanted to say wouldn't come. Maybe that was for the best. So far what he'd said had only made things worse.

'As good as!' she charged furiously. 'I'm really

glad I discovered before it was too late what an intolerant, evil-minded jerk you are!'

His lean profile clenched. She was saying nothing that he didn't deserve. The furious jealousy he had felt when he saw Eve appear with another man had ripped away any claim he had to being civilised. He had never experienced anything like it before, and he never wanted to again.

'Well?'

He arched a brow and said quietly, 'What am I meant to say?'

'Sorry?' she suggested in an icy voice.

'I am sorry,' he said, including Mark in his response.

'Is that meant to make things better?' she shrilled, not to be placated. 'I never want to see you again ever!' she yelled wildly, then, grabbing her brother's arm, she stalked off towards the entrance to her building, not pausing until they were in the communal foyer. 'Is he coming?' she asked her brother through clenched teeth, adding urgently, 'Don't look!'

Mark, who was already looking, turned back. 'Don't worry, he isn't coming. He's gone.'

Eve expelled a long shuddering sigh. 'Gone?' she parroted blankly.

'Yes.'

Mark's smile died as his sister burst into tears.

CHAPTER THIRTEEN

SITTING AT HER desk as Draco walked into the office, his PA beckoned him wildly. 'It's him!'

'I'll take it in my office.' He didn't ask who the him was; there was only one person he had seen make his unflappable middle-aged secretary blush and that was Kamel, the Prince of Surana. He'd be lucky if he got any work out of her for the rest of the day, he thought sourly.

'Hello, Kamel. What can I do for you?'

'Grow a pair.'

It was an answer that only a good friend could have uttered, but even so the harsh suggestion made Draco's eyebrows rise dramatically. 'Have I done something to upset you?'

'You've done something to upset my wife, which amounts to the same thing. No, actually, it's worse.'

Draco, who could only recall having exchanged half a dozen words with the princess at her father's wedding or at the charity evening, waited for an explanation.

'Eve is Hannah's best friend, Draco. They're sisters now! Your name is a dirty word in our home. What the hell is wrong with you, man? Eve is a... Actually, this is none of my business.'

'You're ringing to tell me it's none of your business or that I'm a loser?' Kamel wouldn't be the only one. Josie had stopped asking him about Eve but he could see the disappointment and disapproval in her eyes every time she looked at him.

His best friend, his daughter... Was there a message in there he ought to be hearing...? No, Eve had made her feelings very clear, and, even if he did jump through hoops to get her back, who was to say it wouldn't happen again? There was a limit to how often a man could reinvent himself. He was who he was and if she didn't like him warts and all what was the point?

The point is you're lo... No, he wouldn't even allow himself to think the word. His life was full, busy, and *loneliness* was a state of mind reserved for people who indulged in self-pity.

'Both, but, no, I'm ringing you regardless, and

God knows I hope I'm doing the right thing here…
You know Hannah is pregnant?'

'Congratulations.'

He heard the hissing sound of exasperation echo
down the line at the interruption. 'The thing is the
doctors won't allow her to travel right now and
I'm not leaving her.'

An icy fist suddenly reached into his chest.
'Has something happened to Eve?' On his feet,
he dragged a hand through his hair and thought,
I should be with her.

'Not Eve, no, not in that way.'

'Eve is all right, isn't she? She's not hurt or ill
or…'

'Eve is well. It's her mother, Sarah, who's been
rushed to hospital. We've had Charlie on the
phone and the man is totally distraught, falling
to pieces, as I would be in his place. Sarah has
been admitted with severe pre-eclampsia.'

The medical term rang a warning bell in
Draco's mind. 'That's bad?'

'Very bad,' the other man confirmed. 'Apparently they're going to deliver the baby early to
give her a fighting chance.'

'Charlie told you this?'

'No, Eve did. She took the phone off him and it was just as well as he was sobbing and not making much sense. Hannah is worried sick about Eve, her father, and Sarah, and she feels guilty as hell she can't get there and she's mad at me because I won't leave her and come over to take control of the situation. There's no question that my place is here with her, but if I could tell her someone is there with Eve, and that she isn't alone coping with it all…?'

Draco's jaw tightened. 'I'm the last person Eve would want there.'

'This isn't about you.'

The comment hit Draco with the force of a below-the-belt kick delivered with perfect accuracy.

It was something he had needed to hear. He'd been going through the motions for weeks, telling himself that he was better off alone, but what about Eve, what was best for her? Eve might not want him in her life and the choice was hers, but, *Dio*, he would be a fool not to try to convince her to change her mind. But that was for the future. The priority now was to be there for her, take some of the burden off her slender shoulders.

Halfway out of the door, his keys in his hand,

Draco said to Kamel, 'I'm on my way.' He was about to toss the phone to his secretary when he realised he didn't know where he was going. 'What hospital?'

Every second of the record-breaking fifty-mile journey Draco sat with his jaw clenched and his hands white knuckled on the wheel. He tortured himself with imagined images of Eve alone in pain and distress, having to cope with a disaster that was a whisper away from being a tragedy and having a man far too heavy use her as an emotional prop.

Her mother being in a critical condition was not his fault but everything else could legitimately be placed at his door. His friend thought he was a fool and he was right. If Draco had not been a total fool he'd have been there with Eve right now and she wouldn't be facing this *alone. Alone...* The word kept reverberating through his head.

Well, she wouldn't face anything alone again.

He was going to be there for her whether she wanted him or not. He was not going to let her out of his sight and, short of a restraining order, she couldn't stop him.

That's right, Draco, just bulldoze your way in

because that has worked so well so far! How about showing a bit of humility, saying sorry and letting Eve decide if she wants you there? he told himself.

She'd sent him away but it had been pride and fear of rejection that had stopped him asking her for a second chance. His mouth twisted into a grimace of self-disgust as he caught a glimpse of himself in the rear-view mirror.

'You gutless wonder, Draco.'

She was the best thing that had ever happened to him.

The hospital was a maze of corridors but he finally found someone who could, if not answer his questions, at least show him a visitor's room. The nurse's grave face did not send out a positive message.

If anything had happened to her mother Eve would need a lot of support. It hurt to admit he might not be the person she wanted at such a time, but had anyone contacted her brother?

'Mr Morelli?'

Draco stopped pacing and turned his critical glance on the white-coated doctor who had entered the room. He stifled the impulse to demand to be taken to Eve immediately and tipped his head in acknowledgement.

'Is there any news?'

'You're family?'

It took a supreme effort but despite his frustration at the delay Draco showed no offence at the question. 'I am Draco Morelli. Eve Curtis is my fiancée.'

The younger man's face cleared as he offered a hand. 'Sorry about that but we had an incident earlier. Some enterprising reporter got wind of this and got as far as outside Recovery dressed as a porter.'

'Blood-sucking vampires.'

The medic responded to this heartfelt observation with a nod of his head. 'Unfortunately Mr Latimer's own security overreacted to the situation and we have also had to exclude them. I'm George Robinson, part of Mr Stirling's team. I'll get a nurse to show you to the SCBU. Miss Curtis is with her brother.'

'A boy?'

The doctor nodded. 'Very small, as you'd expect, but his condition is stable. It is the mother we are more concerned about at this juncture.'

In the special care baby unit and feeling very much out of his comfort zone, Draco nodded his thanks when given a gown to put on, and, after washing his hands, he was shown the way to a glass-panelled side room.

The nurse who escorted him was speaking, something comforting, he thought, but Draco, who nodded absently at intervals, was only catching one word in three. His heart nearly stopped when he saw Eve through the glass sitting side on to the door. She was enveloped in the same sort of gown he was wearing, but on her it reached the floor. As he stared she reached forward, her eyes trained on the tiny scrap of humanity in the incubator, attached to tubes and wires that bleeped. The baby appeared smaller than Eve's hand, and the loving expression on her face as she gently touched her finger to the baby's thin cheek brought a film of moisture to his eyes.

Eve heard the nurse enter but didn't take her eyes off the tiny figure in the incubator. Babies should be plump and pink but her baby brother was tiny and wizened, his skin shiny. It looked so fragile that she was afraid to touch him even though they had said that the contact was good for the baby.

'Sorry I let the tea go cold.' Logically she knew the baby couldn't hear her, that his sleep was controlled by the drugs being fed into him and the machines that breathed for him, but she struggled to raise her voice above a whisper. 'He's not in pain, is he?' It didn't seem possible that the tubes protruding from his fragile little body could not cause him pain.

Slowly Eve withdrew her hand and turned her head, her eyes widening when she saw him.

Draco had anticipated many reactions from her and he had as many responses ready. He knew the one he should have used six weeks ago—*he was staying*. But it was the reaction he had *not* anticipated and that he was not prepared for that was the one he actually got.

Something else he was not prepared for was the strength of the feelings that broke loose inside him at the sight of her. She looked so vulnerable and so beautiful that in that second he knew he would have died to save her a moment's pain.

Far better, though, to live for her.

She looked like someone in a trance as she got

to her feet, not shouting at him, not rejecting him, but with a tremulous smile on her face and a glow in her green eyes made even more dramatic by the dark shadows beneath them that sent a surge of relief through him.

'You're really here?' It was like a dream but the past few hours…Eve had no idea how many…had been a complete nightmare.

Unconscious he had said her name, Draco took a stride towards her and with a cry she flung herself at him, her arms going around his middle as her face burrowed into his chest. Draco did the only thing possible: he wrapped his arms around her and pulled her in close to his body as she sobbed and clung to him.

'Just came to say I'm off duty if you—' The midwife, nodding with benevolent approval, took the emotional scene in her stride, having seen many, and left them to it.

'Sorry,' Eve mumbled into his chest. The sobs that had shaken her had stopped but she stayed where she was, leaning heavily into him and unable to summon the strength or the will power to pull free. 'I missed you.'

It was only because the hand stroking her hair

stilled that she registered belatedly what she had said. She lifted her head, too tired to be appalled by what she had admitted and, with her hands flat against his chest, pushed away until she was standing a few feet clear. Head tilted to one side like a curious bird, she angled a cautious look at his face.

Draco stood there holding the red ribbon she had hastily tied her hair back with when she had got the call in the middle of the night; it looked incongruous in his fingers. Unable to shake the idea that if she looked away he'd vanish, her eyes clung to his face, which was crazy. He wasn't a mirage, he was real, and her body reacted to the reality by coming alive... Her nerve endings tingled and her heart began to thud hard.

Draco's presence filled any room he entered, but in this antiseptically white box it was overwhelming but also intensely comforting. She had been feeling desperately alone, unable to stop the negative thoughts filling her head, and weighed down by a terrible sense of impending doom.

And now she wasn't alone... She pressed her hand to her stomach, thinking she was never alone and never would be again. Not the time, not the place, though, so *very* not the place to mention the new life growing inside her when another new life so close by was clinging on so tenaciously to his.

If she hadn't known before, the past few hours had brought home dramatically to her how precious the life she carried was, and how terrifyingly vulnerable. She had never had more admiration than she did now for her own mother, who had carried that responsibility of motherhood alone, had brought her up all by herself.

She would tell her—if she got the chance.

Her lips trembled as she felt tears press at the backs of her eyes. 'My mum might die, Draco.'

The fear shining in her eyes pierced him deeper than a blade. The muscles in his throat worked and the rush of tenderness he felt was so strong it took his breath away. He would have given anything to be able to tell her that nothing bad would happen to her ever again.

He touched the side of her face gently, his fingers brushing over the peachy softness of her smooth cheek before he captured both her hands in his. Drawing them up, he placed them against his chest.

'Why assume the worst when the best could

still happen? Your mother is in the best place and you torturing yourself like this is not helping her, is it?'

Eve swallowed. 'You're right, I know, but—'

'It isn't my mother.'

'No, it's just this place is…' She looked around the room filled with the hum and mechanical bleep of the machines that were monitoring her brother.

'What you need is a break,' he said firmly.

'You can't help yourself, can you?' she said.

He was taking charge again, she thought with a small inward smile. But this time, rather than displaying his usual unstoppable energy, the lines bracketing his mouth were deeper, and those fanning from his incredible eyes were more sharply defined, and his cheekbones pushed tighter than she remembered against his bronzed skin.

'You look tired,' she exclaimed, then winced. 'Sorry, I didn't mean to say that out loud.'

You look beautiful, he thought. 'Hannah sends her love.'

Eve gave a tiny smile and tipped her head in acknowledgement. Hannah's love was good, but it was Draco's love she needed, Draco's love she craved, Draco's love she woke up in the middle of the night feeling the lack of like a big black hole in her chest.

Draco couldn't take his eyes off Eve. There had been moments when he had pictured her pining for him, regretting sending him away. But if she had been missing him it didn't show. Of course the day had left lines of strain around her lovely eyes and soft purple bruises under her eyes but her skin was glowing with health and her magnificent hair was gleaming and glossy.

The feelings Eve had been holding inside for weeks threatened to burst out. She wanted to tell him about the baby, but she tightened her control. This was not the time or place and he was only here because somehow Hannah, from her palace, had asked him to come.

'Have you seen Charlie?' It was odd to be worrying about someone who for so long had been the focus of her loathing, but she was. She had never really believed that Charles Latimer truly cared for her mother, but the first words he had said to the doctors had been, *My wife...whatever it takes, please save my wife.*

He'd said the same thing over and over and he was still with her right now rather than standing over his heir.

Draco shook his head. 'No, I haven't.'

'This is very hard for him.' Fear, she learnt, made her stepfather loud and aggressive, and it was a miracle he had not alienated the people who were trying to help Sarah with his accusations of negligence and dire threats of litigation if she didn't survive.

Eve had had to control her own fear in order to calm him down, and when she'd succeeded his tears and remorse had been in many ways more difficult to cope with than what had preceded them.

'I missed you too.'

The husky words made her eyes fly to his face. If you miss me so much, she wanted to say, why the hell did you go away and not come back? Instead she bit her lip and asked, 'Is Hannah all right?'

'I didn't speak to her.'

Eve suppressed a genuine sigh of relief. When Hannah had rung last, Eve had been feeling particularly emotional and Hannah, who could be quietly persistent, had pushed until the whole story had come tumbling out. It was very possible, she realised guiltily, that her friend had gained quite a one-sided version of the situation.

'Kamel rang and he gave me quite a talking-to. He says she is frantic about you all and very frustrated that she can't be here with you.'

'I don't know why they rang you. You didn't have to come.'

The expression in his dark eyes was tender as he brushed a strand of hair from her face. 'We both know that's not true.'

She stared at him for a long moment and then without a word looked away and retook her seat by the cot, her expression dismissive, her body language distracted.

Typical mixed messages he thought, his scrutiny moving from her remote profile to her fluttery hands. His jaw clenched in frustration. He didn't know what response he had expected but *anything* would have been better than this silence.

Had he not been clear enough?

Did she want him to crawl?

What did she expect?

Maybe a bit of humility?

As quickly as it had erupted his frustrated anger faded. The fact was he would do whatever it took to get Eve back…and, admittedly, his timing was bloody awful.

We both know that's not true…he'd said! If she hadn't forgotten how to, Eve might have laughed.

The fact was she felt she knew nothing, and understood even less! Her head was literally buzzing from lack of sleep and the unremitting stress of not knowing if her mother was okay. Her hormones were all over the place and last but not least was the fact that her secret lay very heavily on her conscience… Draco *might* be saying what she wanted to hear or she could be totally misconstruing a simple kindness.

Eve couldn't trust her own judgement and this was too important to make mistakes and open herself up to ridicule or, even worse, pity!

Draco moved a little closer, lowering his voice as he approached the glass cot with its high-tech attachments. 'How is he?'

'They say he is a fighter.'

It seemed to Draco that he would need to be, but he kept silent. 'How long have you been here?'

'I've no idea,' Eve admitted dully.

'You're exhausted.'

'I'm fine. It's Charlie who's a wreck… He really loves Mum but I never thought he did. I thought he married her because of—' her eyes slid to the incubator '—the baby, but I was wrong, so wrong, about so many things. If Mum dies I'll never be able to say sorry.' Her lips trembled as she blinked away the fresh rush of tears that threatened to overflow from her luminous eyes.

He took hold of the back of her chair. 'Your mum is having the best possible care here.' She turned her head slowly to look up at him, the shadowed sorrow in her incredible eyes wakening every protective instinct he possessed. He just wanted to hold her…for ever.

He touched her cheek lightly with one thumb, curling his hand to frame the side of her face, not touching but close enough to raise the sensitive, fine downy hair on her skin.

'I j-judged Mum because of her affair with Charlie, but I always thought that she had been trapped into it, that she felt she had no alternative. That if she finished with him, she would lose the security of her job and her home. I told myself that was what kept her with him.' She shook her

head. 'It made me feel better about their relationship somehow. Does that sound crazy?'

'It sounds very normal.'

'It never occurred to me to ask her, and we never
spoke about it. It was one of those things she knew
I knew, and I knew she knew I knew...' The sound
of a high-pitched alarm made her flinch and stare
fearfully at the cot, panic building inside her.
'Should we do ...?'

Before she could finish a uniformed figure entered the room. Eve felt the comforting pressure
of Draco's fingers on her shoulder as they watched
the midwife glance at the baby before she pressed
a few buttons on the array of glowing dials and
the noise stopped immediately.

'Is he...?'

'He's fine. All our parents get spooked at first
but after a while they read these things better than
we do. The parents' room is down the hall if you
fancy a coffee or a break. Oh, I'm Alison, by the
way. I've just come on shift and I'll be looking
after...any ideas of a name yet?'

Eve shook her head.

'See you later, then.' The rosy-cheeked midwife angled a questioning look at Eve's face. 'You OK, Mum?'

She didn't trust herself to speak, let alone correct the mistake. It might be a mistake now but in the not so distant future she would be able to claim that tagline...*Mum*.

What if I'm bad at it?

Oh, God, she was so not ready for this!

If I'm not ready, imagine how Draco will feel.

Eve had imagined it; she imagined his reaction a dozen times a day.

She had worked through every possible emotion he might display, every accusation he might fling in the heat of the moment and she had her responses worked out...cool, calm understanding. She wouldn't be hurt; she would be grown up. You're going to be a mother, Eve, she told herself. It's about time you grew up, don't you think?

CHAPTER FOURTEEN

SHE WAS READY and totally prepared.

Every night she had gone to bed thinking she would contact Draco tomorrow, and on the following morning she had woken up and thought of a perfectly valid reason to leave it another day… and on the one day she had actually picked up the phone and dialled his number it had gone straight to messaging. Determined not to wimp out once she had got that far, Eve had rung his office, where she had got through to a particularly superior-sounding female who had left her on hold for what felt like hours and then told her Mr Morelli was not in the office today.

The moment she put the phone down Eve thought of the things she could have said…and *thank you* was not one of them! She had worked herself up into a state of fury, mostly aimed at herself for being so damned meek and not telling that snooty woman where to get off!

Why settle for the messenger? she had asked herself. *Out of the office indeed!* Sure he was! The man should do his own dirty work and someone should tell him that. She had actually got as far as putting on her jacket to go and confront him about avoiding her, when she lost her courage.

She'd have to find it again pretty soon!

'I'm sorry about not correcting that midwife's assumption we were the parents,' she said.

Hearing the tears clogging her voice, he took a long deep breath and exhaled, expelling with the warm air the images the nurse's comment had inserted in his head. As a parent he knew that empathy could take you only so far. Happily Josie had always been a healthy child, but the couple of times she had been really ill…not times he wanted to relive.

Sombre-eyed, he looked at the cot. What if they *were* the parents and this *were* their baby lying there?

'Sorry, I know I should have explained to her but—'

A hissing sound of exasperation left his lips as Draco moved around the chair until he faced her, then, squatting down on his heels, he looked into her pale, unhappy face.

'Will you stop apologising and will you stop imagining everything is your fault? It isn't.'

'Isn't it? I had no idea how Mum felt. I just decided how I thought she *should* feel... I made it up as I went along.'

Draco gave a dry laugh. 'Pretty much like being a parent...I've been making it up for fourteen years.'

She looked at him, her chest swelling with the level of love she felt when she looked at him. 'You're a good father.'

And he would be to their baby too. In her calmer, more rational moments Eve knew that, and she also knew that when he got over his anger and got used to the idea, which might take a bit of time, he would step up.

But Eve didn't want duty; she wanted love.

'I *really* believed that if I could give Mum an option, get her away from him, that she would take it,' Eve admitted sorrowfully. 'It seemed simple then; totally black and white.' She gave a sniff, inviting his incredulity, anticipating his contempt.

Unable to meet his eyes, she continued in husky-throated self-disgust. 'I was such a kid.'

'No, you were and are a daughter who loves her mother very much. Just what is the point in beating yourself up like this, Eve? There comes a point when guilt simply becomes self-indulgent. You are not responsible for what has happened,' he said firmly.

Head down, she gnawed at her full lower lip as she listened. 'Don't make excuses for me; I'm a horrible person.' She lifted her head and scowled at him. 'Why are you smiling?'

'Because you are not a horrible person and even if you were I'd—' He shook his head and stopped, the words *still love you* staying unspoken because if ever there was a wrong time to say I love you, this was it.

'Well, I am. Do you know how many times I've made an excuse not to see her? And when I knew about the baby...' her tortured, self-recrimina-tory gaze went to the incubator where her brother fought for his life '...I couldn't be happy for her.'

'Well, you're here for her now, and you're here for Charlie and the baby.'

She nodded. 'Yes.'

'And it might be a long haul, so why don't we follow the nice nurse's advice—?'

'She's a midwife.'

'The nice *midwife's* advice and take a break?'

'I couldn't.'

'Come on, I'm not taking no for an answer. You need a break.'

'Since when did you ever take no for an answer?' Except when she had told him to go and he had gone, she thought bleakly.

'Then why bother arguing if I'm going to ride roughshod over your wishes anyway?' he teased gently.

She shook her head mutely and looked at the baby. 'He can't even breathe for himself.'

'He doesn't have to. You can't do anything here and they'll let us know if there is any change. Charlie is with your mother. She's doing well.'

'They said that?'

Draco couldn't bear to see the hope in her emerald eyes die. 'I spoke to one of the doctors when I arrived.' However he spun it, what he said would have no bearing on the outcome, and if it made it easier for Eve to bear right now, then as far as he was concerned a white lie was a no-brainer.

'All those tubes and he's so tiny…' Her voice husked with emotion as she compressed her lips and looked away. 'Charlie couldn't even bear to look at him.' The confession came in a rush as she expelled a shaky breath, gulping as she remembered the expression on her stepfather's face when they had asked him if he wanted to see his son. 'And if anything happens to Mum, the baby will be all alone.'

'You can't think that way, Eve.' Emotion roughened his voice.

Her shadowed green eyes lifted; he made it sound so easy! 'I can't not.'

'You mean you *won't*.'

'You make it sound as though I'm enjoying this.'

He looked from her angry, resentful face to her clenched fist and shrugged. 'Hit me if it makes you feel better.'

'Not all of us feel the need to resort to violence!' The remorse she felt was instantaneous at her reminder of his actions towards Mark and she began to mumble an apology but he cut across her.

'He won't be alone—he'll have you and Charlie. The man is just scared right now. Whatever happens, he'll love his son. How could he not?'

'My father didn't love me.' Her tired voice had a sing-song quality as she continued. It seemed to Draco that she had forgotten he was there. 'He wanted Mum to have an abortion and he sent a letter telling her. I found it… I never told Mum. I just put it back. Mum was only a student and she had a holiday job on his estate. He treated her as though she were…and me, I was just rubbish to be got rid of.'

Draco could see it clearly, the girl who had carried the secret of her father's rejection with her into adulthood. The image made his heart ache for her, and awoke his anger. If Charlford were here now…but he wasn't.

He'd died and he was a small loss to the world, to Draco's way of thinking, but it had robbed him of the satisfaction of confronting the man with his desertion…though what good would it have done? He had met the type before and when confronted with their misdeeds they were more often than not incapable of accepting their guilt, let alone feeling any remorse.

He sighed out the anger, and as he looked at Eve he felt an upsurge of pride. 'You were better off without a father like that.'

'That's what Mark said too.'

Suddenly the memories of their last meeting were there between them, seemingly making the air heavy.

'Your brother is not an idiot. Was he all right after I...?'

'He was fine.'

'Good—I said things to hurt you that night.' He gave his head an angry, self-admonitory shake and decided to cut a long story short. 'I was jealous.' It turned out to be easier to admit it to her than it had been to admit the glaringly obvious fact to himself.

Her green eyes widened at the admission. 'That's what Mark said too,' she mumbled, shocked to think what this admission might mean. 'I told him that he was being stupid and that you're not the jealous type at all.'

A ghost of a smile touched Draco's lips. 'You're right, I'm not the *jealous* type *except*, it turns out, where you're concerned.' His stare made her flush. 'I'd like to tell you that I'll never act like that again, but I think if I see you kissing another man I would... Actually I think you can pretty much guarantee I would. You do know you've been driving me crazy from the first moment I saw you.' He stopped and raked a hand through his hair. 'I can't speak of these things in here.'

Eve got to her feet slowly, her thoughts in total chaos. She was confused, shocked, excited. She glanced towards her brother, torn between what she perceived as her duty and her desire. 'I feel like I'm deserting him.'

'It's fine, I understand. I need a break. Can I bring you something…?'

She shook her head and watched him leave, tension translating itself into a rigidity in his normally fluid gait. The door had barely closed before it opened again and the midwife from earlier came in, looking a lot fresher than the colleague she had replaced.

'I've just got some charts to bring up to date and I'll make the little one comfortable. Why don't you go for a break with your man? It can be really hard on them, you know, the ones who keep tight hold of their emotions. The little one won't be alone—I'll be right in here or out by the desk.' She nodded through the glass panel where the nurses' station and its constantly ringing telephone was sited.

Eve stood there for a moment and then nodded, smiling her thanks before blowing her brother a kiss.

Still struggling with the white gown, which appeared to come in only one size—massive—she caught up with Draco outside the parents' lounge, coming out of the door, not into it.

'Aren't you…?

He turned his head and looked at her, and Eve forgot what she was saying; she forgot everything except that he was the most gorgeous man on the planet, the shape of his face, his eyes, his lips, the scar…everything! It seemed unbelievable that there had been moments when she had convinced herself that they were better off apart. When she wasn't lying to herself she had been literally aching for the sound of his voice.

She was aching now, for more than his voice.

She took a deep breath. It was her turn. She leapt into the unknown and the words came in a rush, falling over one another to get out of her mouth before she changed her mind and chickened out.

'When you walked away that day, I felt as if you'd taken a bit of me with you.' She lifted her

hand, intending to press it to her heart to illus-
trate the empty space and let out a squeal of sheer
frustration as the tie on the gown responded to
her impatient tugs by tightening painfully around
her neck. 'Oh, God!' she groaned in a mixture of
frustration and discomfort. 'Can you give me a
hand here? This thing is trying to strangle me…I
can't reach.' Holding the neckline, she couldn't lift
her head to look at him without it digging into her
neck and she let out another squeal of frustration.

'Stay still.'

It was hard to read anything in his voice and his
fingers were steady as they brushed the skin of
her nape. Eve wasn't steady at all; she was shaking and even the lightest touch sent electric shud-
ders through her helplessly receptive body.

'Done.'

Eve kept her head down as she pulled her arm
out of the sleeve. 'I have terrible timing,' she
mumbled as she finally rid herself of the garment.

His lazy laugh was warm and husky. 'I have always found your timing impeccable.'

She lifted her gaze, wanting to see in his face
what she had heard in his voice, but it wasn't there.

Nothing was there. His face was pale and

strangely stiff, his unblinking stare was fixed on…? She glanced downwards.

Realising as she did so that she was wearing her pyjamas, as she had only had time to pull on a pair of boots and throw a thin jacket over the top.

'It might not catch on,' she admitted ruefully, 'but I was in bed when I got the…' Her voice trailed away as it hit her that it wasn't her clothes he was staring at, it was her. Or more specifically the small but definite bump of her belly. For weeks it had been the subject that had dominated her every waking moment and now of all times— she had forgotten.

Slowly, very slowly, her eyes left the soft curve of her belly and when they reached his face they were wide and wary, but there was still nothing to see in his face—nothing. In all her scenarios there had definitely been an explosion…not this… this *nothing*!

Was he even breathing?

The knowledge of what he had been given was totally overwhelming. The life, the life they had made together was growing inside her…and that feeling of total glorious rightness was quickly followed by an insidious fear that spread its roots like a cancer. He had so much to lose, in this place right now, how could that not scream at him? It was all so fragile—this happiness could be snatched away from him at any moment.

'I can see this is a bit of a shock and I understand, but what...?'

His jacket still held the heat of his body as without a word he draped it around her shoulders. He still hadn't said anything to her, and she wondered if that was going to be his response—ignore it and it'll go away!

The knot of hurt in her chest tipped over into anger. 'Aren't you going to say *anything*?'

His muscles along the angular line of his jaw clenched as he carefully closed the door to the sitting room behind him. 'Not in there. I need some fresh air and the people in there at the moment...' His eyes brushed the closed door. Symbolically closing his own internal one on his fear, Draco chose instead to embrace life and love and... He fought down the urge to crush her against him and claim that mouth for his own. 'Need some privacy.'

And I need some answers or questions or both...

She needed something from him; after weeks of not knowing she still didn't know. 'Why?'

He angled a brow and said quietly, 'Think about where we are, Eve. Parents get to make some tough decisions in here.'

'Oh!' Even in her emotional state she had noticed the couple sitting beside an empty cot when she had arrived. Their faces had stayed with her, a mixture of fear, resignation and anger that had fed the sense of dread that lay like a cold stone in her chest.

Unconsciously her own hands went to her stomach where there was a slight but defined bump to curve them around. Her size had resulted in a few raised eyebrows during her recent first antenatal appointment and the phrase *big for dates* had been bandied around. Eve was totally confident that her scan the following week would confirm her dates. There was only one time it could have been, as Draco had always taken care that way. There had just been the one time when the condom had split.

Rather naively she had imagined that one time would be OK.

She tipped her head, her eyes sliding towards

the closed door. It certainly put things into per-
spective. 'All right, but I can't be away from my
brother for long.'

'What I have to say won't take long.'

They were words Eve struggled to take any comfort from as she also struggled to keep up with
his long-legged pace. All the corridors seemed
the same to her, the place was a maze, but Draco
seemed to know exactly which way to head.

Probably in the daytime the gravelled quadran-
gle with its tubs of flowers and benches would be
popular, but not surprisingly at this time of night
it was empty.

As they stepped outside Eve took a deep gulp of
fresh air and looked up at the light-filled rows of
windows surrounding them. She shook her head.

'How do people work here day in and day out,
seeing all that…grief?' She had forgotten the
exact percentage in the recent article she had
begun to read. Eve had scared herself so much
she had stopped halfway through—it had been
about survival rates in very premature births, but
the numbers had horrified her and it seemed that
many very young babies that did survive had long-
term medical problems.

'I suppose there are coping techniques. I imagine they learn to balance compassion with objectivity…and I'm assuming that the good days make it all worth it,' Draco replied.

This was not a good day. 'I was going to tell you about our baby,' she said.

'When?'

'Six weeks ago.'

'That's very specific.' His eyes dropped to her belly. It still hadn't sunk in…*a baby*. A sense of warm anticipation flowed through him as he pictured her with their baby at her breast.

'I rang your office. After they'd put me on hold for ages and they told me you weren't available because you were out of the country…' Her eyes lowered, she recalled the hurt and anger she'd felt, and it was still there in her face when she said with careful neutrality, 'I got the message.'

His eyes narrowed. 'Well, I didn't.'

And the culprit would be the temp who had seemed to feel it beneath her to do anything much but file her nails, and offend at least two clients. It did not surprise him to learn that she had picked and chosen the messages she had passed on.

Did not surprise but did anger him, and he had

already made it clear to the agency who'd supplied her that he had been dissatisfied with her work. The person he had spoken to had been very apologetic, explaining that he was in a difficult position because the temp in question was his wife's sister.

Draco had made the man's position easier by dispensing with the services of his firm.

'When did all this happen?' Draco asked.

'It was Tuesday the sixth.'

'I *was* in the country that day. That's the anniversary of my father's death, and it has become a tradition for us all to go to his favourite spot. We take a picnic, remember him and raise a toast.'

'Oh.'

'So when are you due?'

'Christmas.' She placed a self-conscious hand on her stomach and said defensively, 'I know I'm enormous.'

'You're beautiful, and you'll be a perfect mother.' He had never in his head associated a pregnant woman with sexiness, but looking at Eve and knowing that his child, their child, was growing inside her did not diminish his desire in the slightest; it simply added a new dimension to it.

'Are you all right?' she asked. He was obviously not if he thought she looked beautiful. 'Do you want to sit down?' Looking concerned, she nodded towards the bench that was set against the wall.

He laughed and sat down, pulling her down beside him. 'I would much prefer to lie down.'

The warmth of his hungry, all-encompassing gaze made her shiver. She started in surprise when his hand went to her stomach, curving over the gentle mound.

'And I am the one who should be asking you that question. Are *you* all right?'

None of this was going according to her script. 'I think you might be in shock, Draco.'

'No, I'm in love.' And there was no might about it. 'I thought I had lost you,' he said, his voice thick and unfamiliar with emotion. 'I just lost it when I saw you with Mark. I wanted to kill him! What the hell are we doing living separate lives pretending we can function apart? I can't, I know I can't. I need you, Eve, to be a whole person and not some cardboard cut-out. I need you.'

Eve stared at him, her heart thudding fast, and whispered, 'You don't have to say that.'

'I *do* have to say that,' he countered firmly as

with a smile that made her heart flip he took her wrists and pulled her gently to him. Wrapping her hands around his neck, he kissed her tenderly and with infinite care.

Eve was weeping tears of joy. 'Say it,' she whispered, needing to see it in his eyes when he said the words; then and only then would she allow herself to believe it.

'I love you, Eve. Will you give me a second chance?'

'Idiot!' she said, lovingly touching his cheek. 'Oh, Draco, I've been so unhappy without you. I love you so much.'

With a groan he hauled her to him and kissed her deeply. His smile faded as he drew back and saw the sadness in her eyes.

'What's wrong?'

She shook her head and sniffed. 'It just feels wrong to be this happy at a time like this.'

'Would your mother want you to be happy?'

She nodded tearily.

'Then let's be happy. The real celebrations can wait, but the important thing is we have each other and whatever happens, here or anywhere else, you know I'll be there for you, don't you, Eve?'

Her eyes shone with happiness as she looked into the face of the amazing man she loved so much. 'I do know.'

He kissed her again before they went back in— together.

EPILOGUE

'IT'S SNOWING! IT'S snowing…!'

Josie rushed into the drawing room where her father was placing the angel she had made when she was six on top of the tree. It had lost a piece of wing and the leg surgery had left her lopsided but she always had pride of place.

Eve, looking almost as excited as her stepdaughter, bounced to her feet. 'Snow for Christmas—what could be better?' She gave a contented sigh.

'How about an hour's sleep?' her more pragmatic mate suggested.

'We had three hours last night.' Sleep deprivation had become a way of life but, sleep-deprived or not, her husband was still the handsomest man on the planet and since the birth two weeks earlier he had been at home to help.

She had needed it. Her dating scan, with Draco there beside her, had shown very clearly the reason for her 'large for dates' size. The sight of the two little hearts beating had reduced Eve to tears. Draco said it hadn't hit him for weeks and when it had his reaction had been to go out and buy a house in the country—*as you did*!

'Impulse,' he'd admitted. 'But I drove past on my way to Gabby's and I just thought, I can see our family there—but if you hate it…?'

Eve hadn't hated it, she had loved it, so home for them was now a Victorian vicarage five miles from where his sister lived. Josie was delighted to be so close to her cousin.

During Eve's pregnancy, she and Gabby had grown close and since the birth of her healthy twin sons Gabby had been a real support, as had Josie, who was delighted with her twin brothers. The custody threat hanging over them had gone. Clare had dropped all thoughts of having Josie live with her after she channelled her maternal instincts into her latest project—a donkey sanctuary.

So different from a year ago, when Eve had worked in an empty office on Christmas Eve.

'The snow is sticking—do you think Mum and Charlie will get here?'

They would have a lot of people around the table tomorrow, although Veronica had chosen to stay with Gabby. Their turn to have her next year, she'd promised, but they were all coming over for lunch. And of course Eve's little half-brother Joe, who was now a sturdy little chap who had suffered no long-term ill effects from his shaky start, would be there too. Sarah had spent four days in Intensive Care and there had been times when things had looked very black but she had finally pulled through and had come home a week before Joe.

'They'll be fine.'

Draco came to stand behind her, his hands on her shoulders. Eve leaned back into him, feeling safe, warm and cherished.

'Our first Christmas together... I wish Hannah could come,' Eve said wistfully.

'They'll be here for New Year.'

'I can't wait to see the baby.' Hannah had given birth to a gorgeous little baby girl called Cordelia and she had already asked Eve to be godmother to the baby royal. 'It's so peaceful,' she sighed, staring out at the snowy scene.

On cue the speaker in the corner flooded the room with loud baby squawks.

Eve turned and buried her face in Draco's sweater. 'I shouldn't have tempted fate!' she groaned.

'Davide or Dario?' he asked. Their twin sons

already had very distinct personalities but to him their cries were as identical as their faces and it amazed him that Eve could identify them.

She turned her head and listened for a moment. 'Davide.'

She started for the stairs and he pulled her back. 'No, you sit there and we'll bring them down to you, won't we, Josie?'

Always a willing helper, Josie jumped to her feet.

At the door Draco turned back. A question in her eyes, Eve watched him approach.

'Have I told you how much I love you today?'

She smiled as his lips brushed hers. 'Once or twice,' she murmured against his mouth. 'But,' she admitted, reaching up to frame his face with her hands, 'you can't have too much of a good thing.' And her husband was the *best*!

Coming back into the room to see where her father had got to, Josie rolled her eyes.

'Not again! You're meant to be the responsible adults here. Get a room!'

* * * * *

MILLS & BOON®
Large Print – March 2015

A VIRGIN FOR HIS PRIZE
Lucy Monroe

THE VALQUEZ SEDUCTION
Melanie Milburne

PROTECTING THE DESERT PRINCESS
Carol Marinelli

ONE NIGHT WITH MORELLI
Kim Lawrence

TO DEFY A SHEIKH
Maisey Yates

THE RUSSIAN'S ACQUISITION
Dani Collins

THE TRUE KING OF DAHAAR
Tara Pammi

THE TWELVE DATES OF CHRISTMAS
Susan Meier

AT THE CHATEAU FOR CHRISTMAS
Rebecca Winters

A VERY SPECIAL HOLIDAY GIFT
Barbara Hannay

A NEW YEAR MARRIAGE PROPOSAL
Kate Hardy